C000165480

The Mirrors

by Which

I End

the World

The Mirrors
by Which
I End
the World

Kira Blackwood

EPIC
PUBLISHING

Epic Publiblishing
370 Castle Shannon Blvd., 10366
Pittsburgh, PA 15234
www.epic-publishing.com

First Printing: 2023

ISBN 978-1-7346486-5-2

Epic Publishing is an imprint of Mighty, LLC.
The Epic Publishing Name and logo are trademarks of Mighty, LLC.

To Andrea, the best wife in the world, and to Psycho, the best chicken in the world. I'd gladly share one of my two brain cells with either of you.
Please take turns.

Part One: Empty Skies

Prologue

Michael Sanders's life could be contained in a fourteen by eighteen-inch suitcase, and all proof of his existence could be stowed away in a Chinese food take-out carton. This was just as well because Michael Sanders did not exist. The fact that he did not exist did not stop him from being an ordinary looking man in his mid-twenties who hadn't held a stable job for more than a few months at a time, just as it did not stop his eyes from opening when he heard three car doors shut below his motel room window.

His heart pumped a wave of cortisol and adrenaline through his bloodstream. It was a situation he had become all too used to. He always slept fully clothed, with the exception of his socks and shoes, which were wearing thin.

Through the broken metal slats of his window, he saw the same details he always saw: a black car with tinted windows and no plates driven by men wearing dark, long-sleeved shirts and matching pants, as if dressed in shadow. The street beyond was desolate, the parking lot empty, the sky blank. Neither man nor God would protect him.

He skipped socks, shoving his feet into sneakers, then snagged his toiletry kit from the bathroom sink. He shoved it into the constantly packed suitcase he had left at the foot of his bed. He made sure it stayed packed, ready to grab at a moment's notice, whether to keep him organized for a hasty escape or to use as a blunt weapon if they got the drop on him. The man crouched low, listening to where his would-be abductors were.

The sound of splintering wood came from somewhere nearby as somebody kicked in a door. *Damn it, they're close.* Another slam, this time from the room next door. *They're learning. They split up this time.*

Michael crouched behind the corner of the bed, pressing himself flat against a floor stained by countless former tenants. The doorknob rattled shortly before the door itself exploded inward in a shower of splinters, dust, and rusted hinges. His eyes, which had adjusted to the darkness, focused on the looming silhouette of his latest stalker. A hand wreathed in darkness snaked through the air to the nearby light switch, temporarily blinding him.

Mentally spouting off a string of obscenities, he listened as the soon to be assailant trudged into the bathroom, flicking a switch in there as well. He would only have one moment, one chance to get out of there, but there would be no way of leaving undetected if he didn't make the first move. Michael counted to five and darted from his cover, flicking the lights off.

He heard the alarmed grunt of someone who both was and was not expecting this to happen. He crouched low again as the individual stepped back into the dark room. His attacker would need a moment to adjust from the lights outside to the darkness in Michael's room. That moment of transition was more than enough.

Michael sprang, curling a hand around the man's jaw while using the other to remove the attacker's dark sunglasses. Such affectations, though seemingly pointless at night, were part of The Order's uniform, as they prevented him from using his powers. The man behind the lenses was thick and balding, probably about forty years of age. His skin was sunburned and there was a slight tinge of jaundice in his eyes.

There was no doubt that the attacker had been instructed extensively on why he should never look into the eyes of the man who called himself Michael Sanders, but few who knew of his ability could resist the temptation to see it in action. This curiosity got the better of him.

Connected only by their gaze, the attacker found himself transfixed, trapped in a bluish-black tunnel that seemed to surround them, each staring down the other through a luminescent tunnel. Memories poured from the man, Elijah Johnson, who had a severe drinking problem and had been promised salvation from the emotional struggles that drove him time and time again into the bottle. He was nothing but a lowly acolyte, someone who had been sent along as backup, a disposable bruiser who happened to find their target before the higher-ranked members. Elijah had been assured things would turn out all right in the end; he was an animal that had been brought along as a distraction. Michael couldn't bear the thought of inflicting pain on an individual so lost.

It was easy to grant him the relief The Order emptily promised. Michael felt a familiar sensation flow through him, a tension where there had been nothing before, like steam filling a sealed container, pressure rising, yet not ready to blow. Elijah's face softened, the pain attached to his memories ebbing away like driftwood being brought out to sea. The alcoholic's past became Michael's. Elijah remembered the history, but not the sorrow.

"Now you know they weren't lying." Michael's voice shook as he fought the sadness of a life that wasn't his own. "Get out of here and stay away from The Order." Elijah could only nod as Michael grabbed his suitcase and left. He vaulted over the railing, landing hard, though the cultists were making too much noise to hear his comparably quiet landing.

He reached his car when heavy footsteps came from behind. One set. Male. Moderate size, aggressive. A man Michael had been waiting for. Each abduction regiment had a leader, and tonight, this was the unfortunate soul tasked with taking him in.

Michael spun and delivered a devastating right jab to the bridge of the group leader's nose, smashing cartilage and the plastic frame of another set of sunglasses. The leader found himself slammed into the side of the '98 Volvo Michael had been given a few months earlier. Michael pried the leader's eyelids open, locking their gazes. He unleashed the two decades of alcoholism and emptiness he'd collected from Elijah upon the man, apparently named Herschel; Elijah's pain now resided in this attacker's heart. It would kill him, as it had been slowly killing its original owner. Michael thought nothing of dooming a man who'd condemned so many others.

When Michael looked away, he heard a thud, followed by Herschel sobbing hysterically on the ground. He rolled his shoulders and smiled.

"Thanks. I needed to get that off my chest."

He slid his key into the ignition, the engine kicked over, and Michael barreled down the interstate, heading north along the east coast. A few hours passed with nothing but the dark windows of nearby buildings and long-past-blooming foliage to keep him company. As the sun crested over the horizon, Michael found himself pulling over, parking in a small lot by a beach in Maryland. There were a few other cars there, some with surfboards still strapped to the top. They were unimportant, their owners easily avoided.

Getting out, he retrieved his wallet and other pieces of ID from his suitcase, then got a Chinese food take-out carton from his trunk. A splash of kerosene would ensure it burned up in a minute, tops. He brought his satchel with him.

Crossing the sands to a nearby jetty, its rocky outcropping thrusting back at the relentless crash of the ocean, he sat cross-legged atop the rocks and sighed. That one exhalation was all the mourning he'd allow. He didn't have time to grieve the death of Michael Sanders. Since he was a boy, he'd led a series of short lives punctuated by a sudden burst of flame. He was no phoenix, though. There was no rising from the ashes. He was an arsonist at a masquerade ball, setting fire to his own costumes.

Flipping through alternative identities, he eventually decided on David "Dave" Helmholtz. He then made a few calls: one to Jill Palls, to let her know Michael was returning to California after a death in the family; one to Louis Jorgen, a short order cook at the local diner, to say that he had to leave for Europe due to work; and one to Phillis Glabbern, the motel proprietor, saying that someone had broken into Michael's room, he didn't feel safe and would be heading to Florida.

After this, he snapped the burner phone in two, cheap little flip-phone that it was, and threw it in the Atlantic. After sealing his cut-up driver's license and registration for the Volvo in a take-out container, he shut the lid, tucked the box in between a few boulders, and lit a match. Michael Sanders perished in that flame, trapped inside a tiny cardboard tomb that smelled of soy sauce.

Glancing at a man and woman who were dressed to surf (though they seemed busy tearing each other's wet suits off), he made sure no one else was around. His privacy secured, Dave pulled out a new vehicle registration card and changed the plates, bending the old set in half as a reminder that they could no longer be used. He heard splashing from the waves and knew that the two beachgoers were either awful surfers or great at having sex in the ocean. Dave spray-painted his gray Volvo a pale blue and, with a swift kick, dented the rear side paneling, to ensure people wouldn't recognize his car.

Moments later, he drove away, the giant red sun and burning sky seeming to reflect the endless process of transition in which he'd been caught. An endless road yawning out before him, hours ticking by until, eventually, he found himself in White Plains, a town of roughly seventy-five thousand people along the south-eastern edge of Pennsylvania.

Dave found an affordable apartment building—twelve hundred a month for one bedroom—and dragged his one suitcase to his room. He surveyed the flaking paint, meager fixings, and cracked bathroom sink. This was the nicest place he'd been in two years.

"Yeah…this could work," he mumbled aloud, as if striking a business deal. He took one glance out the window to appreciate the town around him, another into the mirror to take in his bloodshot eyes, and stumbled into the bedroom, letting his eyes shut as fatigue dragged him into the void, where he didn't have to be anyone at all.

Chapter 1

Chelsea Valenti stared out across the sea of drunken, gyrating bodies at Mickey's Sports Bar, her teeth crunching down on another stale pretzel, tongue playing with the crumbs before sending them down her esophagus to their destruction. One half of her agitated mind focused almost obsessively on her looming graduation from the White Plains Institute of Technology, while the other half casually deduced the angles of the architecture, the strength of the support beams, and the average square footage of sitting versus standing room. If you'd asked Mickey's typical patron as to how Mickey could make more money, they would likely have told you that a new decor might bring in a few more customers. If you'd asked Chelsea, she would've said that by moving the bar against the adjacent wall and extending that bar by about six feet, Mickey could double his profits in a month on the increased volume of sales alone. Having more room to move and serve people is kind of important.

Having entered college at sixteen, many professors didn't take her seriously until she proved herself and earned their envious hatred. Others treated her like the only student in class, which led her peers to despise the teenager who showed them up at every turn. Some male students wouldn't go near her, afraid that the law would frown on a grown man so much as talking with such an underage woman, while others couldn't stand anyone smarter than them, leaving her without any romantic attachments, even through graduate school. The female students almost unanimously regarded her as a freak. In fairness, she was set to get her doctorate at twenty-three, so maybe they were right.

"Chelsea! Hey, are you still with us?" A smooth voice snapped the daydreaming woman back to reality. Her head swiveled, turning to face Jordan Garcia, a twenty-two-year-old Latina double-majoring in sociology and political studies. She had a body like a stained-glass window—dazzling from every direction. The two had formed a bond during countless chill out sessions of lukewarm pizza delivered from Shelly's Eatery eaten over the course of a *Dexter* or *NCIS* marathon. Jordan's silken black hair would be tied up in a lazy bun and her curves would be hidden by pajamas or sweats, serving as a reminder to Chelsea that, despite some rumors to the contrary, Jordan wasn't a goddess.

While Jordan seemed to weave through society like a snake through tall grass, Priscilla Aberdeen, seated in the back of their round booth, seemed to take the path of most resistance, whether it was getting decent grades through all night study binges then sleeping through the whole weekend, or dieting by, well, doing the same thing—strict calorie counting and three-hour gym sessions coupled with huge binges. Despite this, she maintained that happiness did not lead to success, and she hadn't gone to college to become a failure.

Next to Chelsea sat Theresa Sillim, who was majoring in religious studies even though she intended to be a full-time yogi, so she didn't need the degree. Her passion gave her a justifiable reason to always wear yoga pants and an athletic top or sweats. It was a style that required little effort to put together, but more importantly, she was always comfortable.

"Hey, Chelsea." Priscilla smiled a little, glancing around with a conspiratorial drop in her voice, as if anyone could've overheard them among the bar's crowd. "Can you do the thing?"

"Oh, yeah!" Jordan grinned, egging Chelsea on. She could

convince damn near anyone to do her bidding with little more than the spark in her eyes. "Do it, come on. Please? For me." She took a long sip of her White Russian, keeping her eyes trained on the soon-to-be-Doctor of Psychology—Chelsea's real passion, despite her skill in mathematics.

Theresa glanced between them, chuckled weakly and joined in. "It's so cool!" She disapproved because it normally meant irritating someone or spoiling a drink. Still, she couldn't stand between her friends and a good time.

Chelsea sighed, masking a smile with a swig of Coke. "What do you want me to hit?"

Jordan pushed the bowl of peanuts her way and glanced around. "Oh, look, Lenny McGuire's here. Poor lonely Lenny. Think you can stick one in his eye?"

Chelsea looked out at the crowd. The bar was oddly crowded, considering it was almost time for the Ghost to strike. People must've moved on from that news cycle. Even serial killers can get boring, apparently.

Looking around the bar, Chelsea couldn't blame people for being out, celebrating the end of the semester. She was out, too, after all. It's natural for people to want to blow off steam. Ironically, the looming threat made people want to go out even more.

Her gaze fell on the disheveled computer engineering major sitting a few booths away, fingers striking on his laptop like pale lightning. He was a junior who'd had to take a semester off for 'personal issues' and hadn't managed to survive falling into the chasm left where his social life had once been.

"Lenny? No, not Lenny…he's nice," she protested half-heartedly, knowing it wouldn't change what was coming. All her training failed her when it came to talking herself out of intense situations.

"Can't do it?" Priscilla teased, a little more sharply than she meant to. Jordan shot her a look. Priscilla turned whiter than playground chalk. "I mean, it's not like you ever get caught, you know? You're every teacher's pet. No one suspects you of anything."

Theresa took a different approach. "Focus, my friend. Center yourself. We talked about this, remember?"

Internally rolling her eyes, Chelsea thought, *Ah yes, the breathing exercises, the balance of one's chakras against the chaos of life, or some such thing.*

Theresa laid her hand on her friend's shoulder. "I believe in you."

"That's…kind of weird to say…but thanks." Chelsea grabbed a peanut.

She surveyed the room, watching Lenny hammering away at his laptop in the center of the crowded room, sixty feet away, with his back to their booth. Her vision flitted across the tables, glasses, ceiling fans, and decorations, calculating the angles between each. Movement speeds, percentiles, and force readings danced through her thoughts, fitting perfectly into her equation. Then, the bartender disappeared into a storeroom, giving her the window she needed.

"Well?" Jordan prodded.

"If theta equals one seven dot one six two…" she trailed off, placing the nut along the back of the seat, "then with a minimal application of force…" She cocked her finger back and flicked. The miniscule projectile bounced off the rim of the raised glass of yet another muscle-bound simpleton, into the spinning blades of the fan above his head, at which point it darted across the room and ricocheted off the edge of Lenny's laptop, directly into his right eye. He let out a yelp, which caused a handful of drunken revelers to glance in his direction.

The man whose glass she'd used in her equation didn't even notice the disturbance. His attention seemed squarely focused on the mounds of exposed flesh popping out of the shirt of the woman at whom he was drooling.

"I knew you could do it!" Theresa hugged Chelsea. Priscilla's face fell as she looked away. Jordan smirked, perfectly happy to sit back and let mayhem unfold as long as she got to push the first domino. *Of course, she's easygoing,* Chelsea thought, never daring to express aloud, *because her sister works for the FBI.*

Chelsea shifted about, feeling her stomach knot as she wondered what Lenny was thinking, or if he knew that she was responsible. Not that he could have. Out of the dozens of times she'd performed that trick, her friends were the only ones who knew the source of the aerial peanut. She'd landed them in shot glasses, the mouths of Tiki statues and unsuspecting strangers, and now, someone's eye.

"I need a drink." She slid out of her seat, standing before her friends could interject. A quick glance at Lenny, who was trying to rub oil and salt out of his eye, conjured a memory of her father standing over her when she was seven and the school had called her parents because she took Dan White's crayons.

"Chelsea," he had said, "what made you think it's okay to do something like that?" When she tearfully attempted to respond, he held up his finger, admonishing her. "It's never okay to hurt people. How would you have liked it if he took your crayons?"

Guilt, to a child, is the end of the world. As it is, they understand little beyond their own environment, and no matter how intelligent Chelsea was, the idea that her parents were angry at her threatened catastrophe. Shaking with uncontrolled sobs, she'd apologized to him, then to Dan the next day, and to her teacher, since she made Ms. Kelly upset. She never stopped being sorry.

Rubbing her eye and shaking her head to dismiss the flashback, Chelsea approached the bar. She spent a moment glancing over the bartender, whose most striking characteristic was that he seemed to look exactly like everyone else despite his blue eyes and messy, medium-length hair. While not unattractive, he was far from the best-looking guy around, though something in how he carried himself held her attention for a little longer than she intended. His face, as far as she knew, never moved, never betrayed what was going on in his head, much like *The Thinker*. What he was thinking, no one was sure, but he seemed to always be thinking about something terrible. Who was going to waste the time of a man who looked so forgettable, yet so tense?

"Another Coke?" he called out to her, his rough voice breaking through the din around her. It sounded rough and smooth at the same time in an impossible way. Sandpaper covered in oil.

"Uh, yeah, thanks." She nodded vehemently to make sure he understood. Dropping a few crumpled bills on her tiny corner of the bar, she watched as he pulled a small, red can out from behind clinking rows of Bud Lights and other assorted intoxicants. She unknowingly rolled her eyes, unable to figure out why so many people seemed eager to guzzle what most studies and autopsy reports indicated was poison.

He approached her, holding out the drink, his stone face still set in its serious expression. Their eyes locked and she felt transfixed for a fraction of a second. His forgettable eyes almost...glowed. Despite how ordinary they were, she felt totally, physically captivated. As she curled her fingers around the can and tried to pull away, she found that he was still holding tight.

"By the way, we prefer our snacks to stay out of peoples' eyes."

Her heart stopped, and her eyes went wide. The world fell away, leaving her alone with the too-serious bartender with moss green eyes, ancient spherules that reflected a thousand years of lost wisdom. No wonder he was the one to catch her. Everyone else looked, but something in her gut told her this man could *see*, and he did, in fact, see her. Now she was screwed and about to get kicked out of her favorite bar, which she loved even though she didn't drink. That meant buying soda from the 7-11 and drinking in her dorm, alone, like an undergrad.

Then, the twenty-something's stone face cracked a wry grin, his calloused hand releasing her drink. It nearly tumbled from her hands, but she managed to compose herself before anything disastrous happened.

"Nice shot, though."

"T-thanks, Dave," she whispered, unable to speak louder.

The enigma known as Dave the Bartender defied her considerable deductive powers. She knew nothing of him, other than that he came to White Plains a few months ago, nor could she derive any details from his clothing, demeanor, or personality. Everything about him seemed to be the most ordinary possible choice. That smile was a clue to something, but she didn't have enough information to make it meaningful.

Chelsea wondered if 'exceedingly ordinary' could be a clue. Nobody looked that plain by accident. Maybe Dave didn't want to be noticed—but that smirk, lording his strange knowingness over her, suggested he couldn't resist showing off. Some kind of gift, maybe?

Dave appeared to like certain kinds of attention, though he hated being noticed. Even as the bartender, he made sure to never command the room...which likely meant a traumatic past, or he was on the run. Or both.

But still, how did he catch me?

She wove her way through the crowd but was so perturbed by his having caught her that, for once, she didn't stop to think enviously of the buxom, flat-stomached women lining the room. It wasn't as though Chelsea didn't have her own 'assets,' but having extra weight around her middle (albeit, only a little extra) made potential suitors hard to come by, especially if Jordan was around. Food filled a void that had always lurked in the center of her heart, swallowing her up when she allowed her mind to wander.

"What's wrong?" Priscilla asked, scrutinizing Chelsea as soon as she sat down.

"N-nothing, why?"

"You're so pale. Are you well?" Theresa placed a palm against Chelsea's forehead, though it was quickly slapped away.

"I'm fine!" Chelsea cried, watching her friends draw back in surprise. She sighed, and then looked over at them, still reeling. "Dave saw me."

"Saw you? With the peanut?"

"No way!"

"Oh, dear!" came the chorus of hushed murmurs.

"Yes...with the peanut..." She began to trail off as she attempted to figure out how the man could've caught her. *Hadn't he been in the back room?*

"How?"

"Was he mad?"

"Do we have to leave?"

"No, he...fine..." she mumbled absently, trying to review which mirrors and security cameras were placed where, and if it was possible, he'd been tipped off by a phone call or text message, or if another patron, perhaps, had—

"Hey, stay with us!" Jordan snapped, bringing Chelsea back to attention. "It's ladies' night, and we're celebrating. No zombies allowed."

Chelsea forced herself to laugh, both insulted and charmed by Jordan's comment. She couldn't deny that she tended to zone out when something really captivated her interest, usually to the point she'd forget homework and miss meals. During one particularly intense semester, she'd gone into 'zombie mode,' as Jordan called it, frequently enough to convince her friends that she'd become anorexic, often forgetting to eat, once for over a day. She lost seventeen pounds before her friends staged a three-hour intervention. She was able to persuade them she wasn't anorexic, just distracted. Mostly. They kept a wary eye on her for a while, but she loved them all the more for it.

"Relax, I'm with you, it's just..." She bit her lip, finishing quietly, hoping they might have insight to his knowledge. "He wasn't even there."

"What was that?" Theresa looked over.

Chelsea glanced between her friends, meeting their eager

eyes, wondering what was running through their minds. Something told her not to mention that little connection she and Dave shared, when his gaze went straight through her and, for the briefest instant, warmed the chill that had lingered in her soul for so long. He'd connected with her. It felt like she could've told him anything, and Dave would have been happy to take that pain away. But how? He'd done that with his stare. He'd done something impossible.

She just didn't know what.

"Nothing." Flashing a grin, she rose from her seat and made for the door. "Listen, I told my folks I'd head out to their house for a little bit."

"Aw, come on, stay a little longer! For me?" Jordan smiled cheekily, showing off her teeth. There was a slight gap in her dental structure, the only flaw grounding her on Earth with the other mortals.

"Sorry, tomorrow's reading day, and I promised them I'd hang around and spend some quality family time."

"Good thing you don't study, Dr. Valenti." Priscilla pouted, pretending she said it as a joke, only fooling herself.

"But we're having fun! We barely ever get to come to the bar anymore. When you graduate, I imagine we'll have even less time together." Theresa slumped onto the table, staring at Chelsea with giant, shimmering eyes.

"We can come here any time. That's what finals week is for, right? Pound out a test, then a few drinks, and repeat?" Chelsea called over the growing din.

"Who gave you that crazy advice?" She laughed. "Your parents would worry, huh?"

"Precisely." Chelsea smiled, eyes lingering on her friends. They laughed and waved as she slipped out into the starless night.

Chapter 2

To date, Theodore "Theo" Jotun had overseen the deaths of twenty-two sacrifices. It was time he picked number twenty-three.

At his computer, he began searching his usual criteria: adult female, brown-ish hair, plump but not heavy, dark eyes, and living with her family somewhere in New York, New Jersey, or Pennsylvania. He discounted those who were overly masculine, those who were emotionally secure, those who had excessively large families, and, after some screening, smiled at the image before him. A Facebook profile showed him all he needed: where she lived, what bar she went to most, what school she went to, and best of all (the only part he really needed), her name. All his skill as an FBI profiler went into identifying the perfect victim.

He glanced at the Special Agent badge on his desk and scoffed. The Bureau never made him feel as validated, nor as powerful, as his *real* job. Theo rose from his desk, stretching his arms overhead, fingers almost brushing the low ceiling of his modest office. Lamps glowed in the corner—he hated overhead lighting while trying to work. Without windows, he could utterly lose himself in his pursuits. His office sat several stories underground, after all.

Theo's hands brushed along the worn leather of the tome on his desk. Emblazoned upon the surface were the words he defined his whole adult life by: *The Saint of Glorious Pain.* His grandfather passed the book on to him, after years upon years of studying its pages, trying to determine from whence it came, and to find the civilization that worshipped this 'Saint.' That search ultimately killed him.

A smile crept across Theo's face. Soon, the book would become irrelevant. The Saint of Glorious Pain, referred to in the book as Nyoru, did not exist in their world...yet.

Anyone looking hard enough could find whispers of other Saints. Brutal and bizarre deaths, hinting at the presence of something beyond human walking the earth, reported on the news as 'accidents' or 'mysterious circumstances.' Forums on the dark web had hundreds of followers dedicated to investigating these beings, the way some still hunted for Bigfoot or the Loch Ness Monster, except these Saints truly existed. Only a few so far, but more and more as time went on, it seemed. Once content to be spirits, they were now becoming incarnates, born into flesh, or transforming an existing body, to walk the human plane.

Reality grew thinner by the day, and strange beings were creeping through the holes.

Theo picked up the tome, eyes lingering on a picture of himself and his family. What his family used to be. His wife stood at his side, cradling their infant son. Both long gone from his life by now.

With a grimace and a twang in his heart, he left his office, making his way through dull concrete corridors to the main hall in basement level one. Each hall would've been the same, if not for the art hung throughout their tunnels. Stake burnings, ritual sacrifices, crucifixions, flagellations—if it showed a human in the thralls of ecstatic suffering, it found a place in these corridors, hung to remind his flock of their divine purpose. Humankind always worshipped pain, just never admitted it. All of history had been marked by the ash and blood of those tortured to reveal their true selves. Every great society thrived on the agony of its masses.

He heard the throng of his followers murmuring, waiting, falling into rapt silence as he took his place at the podium. It stood on a raised platform, and this room had perhaps the most compelling art of all. Rather than paintings, this room had photographs. While many of their order received physical torment as reward for their worship and as punishment for their transgressions, the chapel held photographs of each sacrifice he'd made to Nyoru. Every woman Theo had personally identified, captured, and tortured, prolonging their pain as long as possible to appease the Saint, ensuring a swift return. One woman danced on hot coals until she collapsed, very slowly burning to death. Another, he'd run through with metal spikes until she begged to die. Though each photograph captured him standing over the lamb he'd brought to slaughter, none captured the screams echoing off the walls of their subterranean prison, more devout, more sincere, than any prayer they ever said for mercy.

As Grand Master of the Order of Nyoru, he held command at the front of their chapel, a room long enough to seat the important members of their congregation. The others kept to their rooms, studying the texts, preparing to be acolytes to Nyoru, once they birthed their god into a human form.

To keep out of the public eye, they operated out of remote safe houses and, primarily, an underground headquarters. Members were forbidden from speaking about their activities to non-members or posting about their activities on any public forum. They had special cells, and an entire building, in fact, for those who broke these rules.

"Loyal followers," he said, cherishing the echo of his voice off the back wall, "thank you, as always, for joining me. I come bearing little news, and what I share today, I do not share with pride. The Vessel continues to elude our pursuit despite our best efforts to bring him back into our midst. Due to this failure, I have identified the next sacrifice, that we may appease the Saint of Glorious Pain until its return to the physical realm. We, as those who know the value of suffering, and openly delight in its administration, are more honest than any other human. We are true to the craving for violence that lurks in every person's soul. So long as we continue to show our worship, then upon the incarnation, we will reign over those who flee from the truth that all religions know: life is pain; from pain comes knowledge; from knowledge comes control over those who lack it. Were Adam and Eve damned for disobedience, or because they, too, could now command the beasts?"

Theo paused to let this sink in, cherishing the way their greedy eyes stared up at him, desperate to be acknowledged. That's how he recruited most of these people: stalking the dark web to find the most pathetic and vulnerable, then offering them a cause worth dying for.

"As such, I read today from the prophecy of Nyoru's return."

He flipped through the yellowing pages until he found the passage about Nyoru's return. "Here it is written that, when mankind is in its darkest hours, the world will not end, as other religions prophesize. No, in this time, when all of humankind has turned to fear, and anguish is at its highest, the Saint of Glorious Pain will return, split in two, as its power is too immense to channel directly into a single mortal form.

"Humans are frail. Weak. Selfish. Our bodies cannot withstand the process. This is why the Vessel holds Nyoru's power—that of Transference, of taking the darkness of pain that roots in our hearts, replacing it with joyful, peaceful light. In return, the Saint will inflict that which he takes onto others. It is the duty of the Vessel to use this power, despite the suffering it will cause him, to let the power mature. When this happens, it will be shared with the Incarnate, the being whose flesh can endure ascension to its true status. Once merged, the being will become Nyoru, and upon returning to the mortal realm, the Saint of Glorious Pain will be free, empowered fully in our reality, crossing at will between the physical and astral realms, ready to unleash upon all the Earth such wonder and such agony that none who cross the Saint will survive.

"Until such a time as our god returns, it is our duty to embrace suffering. Others preach about the end of suffering, an attempt to find peace and solace from the torment mortality wreaks upon our souls. But, if the world is full of suffering, is it not right to think suffering is the natural state of all beings? Is it not folly, then, to resist pain, and hide our wounds, when we could, in fact, accept them, bearing our scars with pride? Does it not bring further pain to dwell in shame and misery, when accepting your wounds brings you strength?"

A ripple of excited agreement passed over the crowd. Groupthink and buzzwords kept a lot of them from asking questions he didn't want to answer, like, *If we know who the Vessel is, who is the Incarnate?*

"Go then, loyal followers, and writhe. Do unto yourselves as the early Catholics knew to be right. Fast. Beat yourselves. Burn and cut and whip your untested flesh. Bleed and scream for the Saint of Glorious Pain, so, upon its return, our god may see the wounds on your body and the scars in your mind and reward you for your dedication. Accept suffering, so upon Nyo-ru's return, your pain can become your power over all those who have offended the Saint by fleeing from their own torment into the fugue of medication, vice, and, worst of all, comfort.

"And remember." He smiled. "If you are unable to show dedication to suffering on your own, then, to ensure proper worship, a partner will be assigned to inflict suffering upon you. Such is the word of the Saint of Glorious Pain."

In response to this final ministration, his followers all rose, speaking in unison. "Ascension through agony, so speaks the Saint."

The Grand Master grinned. None of them were allowed to read from *The Black Tome*, so they didn't know the truth: that the Vessel would be inexorably drawn toward the Incarnate. The Vessel knew this, felt the tug, and thus, always knew to flee in the other direction, but his followers had tracked the man to

Maine and Mexico and even Singapore. He could not escape giving his power over to Theo. The book, this religion, had all chosen him. As the one destined to ascend to Sainthood, he held the full power and authority of a god lurking inside him, waiting to be unleashed.

The family he no longer had loomed in his memory, and he grimaced, shaking the memory away as he returned to his office. Once there, he set the photo face down, but couldn't bring himself to hide it away. Not today. Her suicide, the loss of his child—he couldn't ignore that, just as he never shied away from the fact that, after the Transference, both he *and* the Vessel would have the Saint's power, so he'd have to kill the Vessel to maintain his status unchallenged.

After the sermon he'd delivered, it wouldn't be fitting of one like himself to turn away from these facts, no matter the pain they may have caused him. It didn't matter in the end. He only needed to convince the Order to follow him for long enough that he could secure his true power. After that, they could, and would, all perish.

Caring for these frail creatures is a waste of time. The lost cannot be recovered, and the vagrant souls that live here are beyond all hope. What use are these flawed creatures to me?

Chapter 3

"Let go, you're killing me!" Chelsea laughed as her father, Jack Valenti, swung her through the air, arms wrapped tight around her soft frame. Pauline, her mother, watched, a warm smile stretching across her wrinkled face.

"Aw, I'd never do that to ya, pumpkin," Jack chuckled, setting her down.

She sucked down an exaggerated gasp of air, collapsing against the wall behind her. Her father may have been sixty-two but weighed a little over two hundred and fifty pounds and had no discernible body fat. Accented by the stubble he'd accrued from only shaving once a week and his deep, booming voice, his visage had the intimidation factor of Schwarzenegger, pre-political career.

If anyone can lift me, it's him. She looked around to avoid her parents' overly affectionate stares.

"I made your favorite, *Doctor* Valenti!" Pauline beamed, clasping her hands together over an off-white, grease-stained smock as her eyes began to moisten.

Oh, please don't cry. I hate it when you cry, Chelsea thought, her mind spinning back to all the things she'd never said for the sake of not seeing those tears. "Thanks, Mom." Chelsea smiled wearily, hoping to cut her off before the waterworks began. "Just let me put my belongings away. Then I'll be ready to eat, okay?"

"Take your time, sweetheart," her father said, his deep voice once again giving her the impression that her father was a bear, though he was more of a teddy bear than anything else. "Do you need help with your bags?"

"Don't worry, Dad, I've got it covered." She smiled only until she had her back to him.

The Valenti family was a simple one, and their house was equally so. A few pictures lined the main hallway of their modest, ranch-style home, but they were all of family. The few pieces of art that could be found in the house were all signed 'Pauline Valenti.'

The house reminded Chelsea of her childhood. Of days spent going in and out of classes that weren't nearly challenging enough for her. Of nights spent in her room crying as she fought to recover from the jeers and catcalls of people who refused to leave her alone. Of years spent trying to convince herself that she *was* good enough and that it *was* okay to be smart and that a great job would make everything worth the pain.

But her mind had decided that recovery was not going to be a simple process. Each word became a wall, each insult another dead end, until she found herself in a labyrinth of memory, praying she could escape before the Minotaur could run her through. Being home was nice, but it made her feel like she'd never be able to get out.

Her home's walls were a slightly faded beige, the floors were neat, the tables still had the same cloths covering them, and her parents stared at her with the same unwavering support they always had.

As Chelsea predicted, nothing had changed. *Nothing ever changes.*

Once back in her room, she changed out of her cotton skirt and blouse, choosing to don sweats instead. They were far from her dressiest outfit, but she knew her parents wouldn't object. The happy, sunshine-filled bubble they lived in couldn't be burst by their daughter's choice to abandon any sense of fashion. Besides, home is supposed to be the one place you can dress like crap and not have anyone tell you off for it. At least, it's supposed to be.

She made the mistake of glancing into the mirror while changing, inevitably locking eyes with her reflection, getting lost along a reflective train of thought. By all friendly accounts, she looked fine, but having gone her whole life without much more than a second date left a lot of room for doubt. She didn't mind dating. She just never cared much for getting...physical. The few guys who ever showed interest in her really only wanted her for one thing, and if they could've stripped her like a totaled car and had their run with the parts they wanted, they probably would've done so. Even those creeps were rare. The fact that nobody seemed interested in *her* made Chelsea wonder what was driving people away.

In truth, the issue ran deeper. She approached the mirror, lifting a hand to rest gently against the glass. She looked into her own eyes. The emptiness she had felt her whole life seemed all the worse when face-to-face with herself. Maybe imposter syndrome. Maybe a touch of depression. Possibly a little trauma from K-12 bullying. Whatever it was made her feel broken, or worse, somehow monstrous, like she didn't deserve a seat among her friends.

Her pupils always felt so abyssal, vacuous, and black. She was the one staring, and the one staring back.

Tearing the scrunchie from her hair, she shook out the light-brown strands and let them fall haphazardly about her face. But she couldn't go to dinner in an angst-ridden huff, so Chelsea shut her eyes and took a few deep breaths, trying to imagine negative energy leaving her body as smoke or steam or whatever the hell Theresa usually said.

The cool floor sent a tiny chill through her legs as she padded out to the kitchen, where her mother had set out steaming plates along a metal-topped island in the center of the room. A bowl of roasted Brussels sprouts sat beside mashed sweet potatoes and a large cut of salmon baked with a mango salsa coating. Chelsea smiled. Laid out before her was, in fact, her once and future favorite meal, one that she hadn't been able to enjoy recently due to her lack of having a stove at her university housing.

"It's fresh out of the oven." Pauline beamed, as happy to have her daughter home as she was about providing a meal for her family.

"Always is, honey. I don't think you've put dinner out too late or too soon in twenty-seven years." Jack nodded approvingly.

Amazing. Simply amazing. They've been together for longer than I've been alive and still enjoy each other's company. Where does that come from? It's like there's something different in their brains that enables them to simply love themselves, love each other, love without question or expectation. What in them allows them to be so…carefree? Or what is it that I lack?

"Hey, pumpkin." Her father waved his hand across her face. "You there?"

Chelsea drew back, finding herself off guard as she was thrust from daydream to reality with enough force to leave mental whiplash. For a moment, her eyes widened, and her mouth gaped uselessly, her tongue having been disconnected from her brain. Jack and Pauline exchanged a worried glance.

"Yeah, just…thinking." Her stilted, awkward recovery didn't hide much, but she crossed her fingers in the hope that they wouldn't pry.

"Okay," came her father's careful response.

Why are they being so strange? Do they know something?

"So, how has school been? We haven't gotten to see you lately." Pauline's eyes darted between Chelsea and the Brussels sprouts she was serving.

"I know, I'm sorry. My dissertation and all. Very time consuming."

"What were ya writin' it on?" Jack cocked his head while shoveling fish and potatoes into his mouth. "Sorry that I don't remember it jus' right, honey, but all that, uh…"

"Technical wording?" Chelsea finished. Jack nodded, smiling unabashedly as his daughter gave a light laugh and took a bite of salmon.

A simple man, but he knows it. Must be nice.

"I'm writing about the adaptive neurocognitive processes involved with limbic system stimulation, assessing resilience in the face of emotional distress, and why some incidents lead to trauma while others do not, with a hypothesis that empathy, both given and received, allow the subject to become better at tolerating distress in the future."

"There's our little genius," he boomed so loudly that the women winced. "Uh, so what does that mean?"

She swallowed. "Well, basically, everyone reacts to stuff differently. Everyone has different activity levels, different behaviors, different ways of coping. So, it's my theory that those who are more capable of understanding the difficulties of others are therefore able to tolerate difficulties themselves."

"And…that would let us…" Pauline squinted, as if an explanation might be written in the air in front of her but was too faint to see.

In full, ideally, prevent PTSD, lessen anxiety disorders, avoid incidents of violence, and generally improve the world. "Keep people off drugs." A partial answer, but still true. Her parents weren't big picture people.

"Imagine that! You'd be a lifesaver," her mother gushed.

"We're so proud of you, sweetheart." Jack smiled.

Chelsea smiled back, but she could feel her cheeks scrunching up. It was an unavoidable indicator of her emotional state, so she took another bite before her parents' prying eyes could notice. The room settled into a silence that was disturbed only by the sound of chewing.

"You know what you are? You're like a bull, except, you know, with your brain," Jack mumbled through another mouthful of food, tapping his temple with his fork.

"…What?" Chelsea cocked her head.

"You charge forward all the time. It's like you see something you want, and you go for it because you can. You've got the brains to do anything you want; all you need is the right tools to get the job done."

"Thanks, Dad." She chuckled, knowing he meant well. "I'll keep that in mind."

"Hey, you might think this is just your dad being a goof, but seriously. You're a bull. Don't be afraid to use your horns."

Chelsea looked up into her father's eyes. He'd stopped eating to make that statement, so she nodded. "Okay, Dad."

With that, he dove back into his meal, having seemed to already forget the brief and unusually serious interruption.

"Oh, I'm so glad you're back, honey." Her mother clasped her hands together. "After you've finished your tests and moved out of your room, we'll get to bake-bake-bake the night away, like when you were little! Won't that be fun?"

The young almost-doctor thought back on the long hours spent baking, on the jokes and laughter she shared with her mother—and no one else. She'd walked a lonely road for many years and didn't see it ending any time soon. If anything, the twists and turns had gotten sharper, the hills steeper, and the world colder.

"Yeah." Chelsea smiled wearily. "Sounds fun."

Chapter 4

Theo sat behind his oversized desk, his fingers tented over his lips as he stared down another glass of scotch, savoring the way it burned his throat. The drink wasn't helping his brooding disposition, but he gradually unfolded his hands and brought the glass to his lips. Alcohol granted a permissible escape from pain because the discomfort of a hangover, especially a severe one, would be its own holy rite. The ticking of an antique clock and the hum of the slightly out-of-date Mac beside it were the only sounds to disturb his quiet self-destruction. Valenti would have to wait. Tonight was all about the Vessel.

Between him and the computer were a few clues to his objective, though they weren't helpful. A discarded granola bar wrapper. The number to a no-longer-used burner phone. The name of a diner he used to frequent. None of these had turned up any leads on where he might have been going. They were dead ends. The Vessel was, as always, a ghost, fleeing the mandate of his existence.

Theo rested his palm against his head, wondering where the man formerly known as Michael Sanders had gone this time. Though the Order, guided by Theo's FBI training, was great at finding him, the Vessel knew how to cover his tracks. The acolytes nearly had him cornered last time, but something had gone wrong, and that snake slithered off to more anonymous prospects.

Last time, he'd been spotted heading east from Nashville along a stretch of highway, and a gas station attendant pointed one of his men in the right direction. The time before, a pay phone call to yet another former boss confirmed he'd gone south after leaving Chicago.

Theo sighed and reached into the bottom right drawer of his desk, pulling out a half-empty bottle of a single malt he didn't bother to learn the name of. The heat in his cheeks egged him on. A pop of the cork leaving its bottle preceded the sacred melody of alcohol filling his glass. He set the bottle down without bothering to cork it.

The door cracked open and Harmony Sharp, an albino as well as one of the younger women he worked with, poked her head in. "Grand Master? May I speak with you?"

The Grand Master shook his head, trying to straighten out his vision. So often, so many countless times, he thought of her as a ghost, knowing she wasn't the only spirit haunting him.

"I understand." She turned to go, her heels clacking like bones against the tile floor, but he told her to wait. Stopping, the woman turned back, her delicate white hair spinning about her shoulders like wisps of fog, some strands falling over her eyes, obscuring her pale red irises. "Yes, sir?"

"Sorry, I…didn't mean to send you off. What is it you wanted to say?" He blinked, his gaze eventually settling on her bone-thin body. Part of him wondered why she dressed in white jeans, a long-sleeved white shirt and white shoes every day, but he didn't make it his business to question such things unless it became necessary. Sometimes he referred to her as the Bone Woman, but only in his head.

"The…The Vessel…I believe I spotted him on a You-Tube video, in the background of cell phone footage from a bar in White Plains, Pennsylvania. I thought you'd like to know. I mean, I might be wrong, but we don't have leads, so I figured…" She trailed off, biting her lip. Her hands were clasped in front of her, and she looked at the floor. Harmony was a newish recruit. Most of the new members were brought in by lower ranking members. Not her.

Theo's head spun, as much from shock as from intoxication. She only went through the most cursory investigative education. *Is it possible? Did this skeleton truly trounce my higher officers? Through YouTube, of all the damn things?*

"Would you like to see the footage, sir?" Straight-backed, unfalteringly respectful, and soft spoken, Harmony was his perfect servant. His right-hand. He felt an odd kinship around her.

"Hey, loser. Where'd your mom go? She leave 'cuz you creep her the hell out?" echoed another schoolyard taunt. *"You gonna cry again? Go on, cry!"*

Though decades old, the jeers etched themselves on his heart. Grandfather raised him because both his parents left. His father, before birth, and his mother a few years after. He knew now that the pain of their absence primed him for his ascension. Each became a necessary suffering, and one step toward his Sainthood. When he married a woman and had a child, he took another step. When he lost his wife, when his son abandoned him, he took a few more. Pain, after all, becomes power, if used correctly.

He focused, making sure not to slur his words as he followed her example, straightening up and smoothing his shirt. Taking a few steps toward her, he made eye contact, holding her gaze, then lifted his hand to hold her chin.

"When I first met you, I saw a girl who wasted her life on a sociology degree—a floundering miscreant who taught herself to crack firewalls like eggshells, an orphan with a dwindling trust and no career who couldn't get a job because society couldn't get past her skin. Beneath all that trauma, I saw potential. A bright, gifted, tortured genius. Might I say, dear, what a great addition to our family you are."

Theo finished with a gentle kiss to her forehead, striding quickly down the hallway with Harmony hurrying to follow in his footsteps.

Chapter 5

A week later...

Dave Helmholtz suppressed a yawn and scanned over a shelf stacked with canned beans and ramen noodles, thankful for the semester having ended. He'd found that, if class was in session, those grubby college students couldn't keep their paws off the just-add-water and pre-made meals in MegaFoods. This left little for him to eat, since he wasn't in the habit of making food himself.

Something caught his eye at the end of the aisle. Glancing up, he noticed Chelsea perusing the mustard selection. In the proper, non-bar lighting, he could see her blotchy complexion, even though she often wore foundation to smooth her skin tone when at the bar. He opted to ignore her and snatch an armful of things he could eat without needing a microwave. Moving through the store on autopilot, Dave grabbed a case of water, some granola bars, and miscellaneous fruit while ducking around the parents who found their phones more important than their children. A glance at his watch read 2:45 PM. He didn't start work for another four hours.

Cursing himself for waking up earlier than he had to, Dave got into line. Chelsea pulled up next to him with a cart of eggs, buns, meats, and other perishable goods he would never have bought. Dave snapped his head forward.

Maybe she won't recognize me. I mean, she saw me a few times, but in a dark room, with lots of people around and she had a few drinks—

wait, damn, she only drinks Coke.

"Hey, Dave, right?" Without moving his neck, he flicked his eyes to the side, catching sight of Chelsea. The lights overhead buzzed and flickered, intent on giving migraines to everyone in the building.

"Uhh, yeah. Hi. You're…Donna, right?" Fumbling deliberately, he hoped he could simply drive her off with the 'typical stupid, shallow guy who doesn't remember women's names' routine, but she didn't buy it. However, her eyes sharpened slightly. She knew what he was doing.

"Chelsea. Not used to seeing me in actual light, huh?" she teased. "How've you been? Planning a trip?" She pointed to his cart, which had enough non-perishables to make it to Juneau.

Too many questions would get someone hurt, no matter what answers he gave. He shook his head. "Yeah, I'm skipping town in a few days. Heading south though, maybe New Orleans if nothing stops me along the way. Gotta get out there, you know? Take a road trip. See the world. Don't want to grow old slingin' whiskey." He looked over the newspapers, pausing on a headline that screamed *MURDERER STILL AT LARGE.*

"Oh, really?" She smirked. Chelsea wasn't falling for it, but hopefully would think he liked playing hard-to-get. He was a professional at that game, but not by choice. "Well, have fun not-cooking, Dave."

Before turning away, he glanced over her, compelled to say something. Ninety-nine percent of everyone he met could vanish into obscurity, but he couldn't shake the feeling he had to say something. Against all logic and every survival mechanism he'd perfected over the last decade, Dave cleared his throat.

"What are you shopping for? Party?"

She turned back with a smile that said, *I knew you'd keep the conversation going.*

"Yes, my birthday. Parents sent me out to pick stuff up while they tidy the place."

"Oh? How old? Twenty…seven? Eight? I know you have

a doctorate, right?" He began unloading his items as they talked between aisles. For all he knew, there wasn't a cashier at either of their lanes, since his gaze was focused entirely on her—and not for his usual reasons.

"Three. Twenty-three." She looked away, rubbing the back of her head with a practiced faux humility, trying not to smile.

"A doctor at twenty-two? Really? You must be really smart, or hardworking. Or both." Dave took out a wad of tens and twenties, sliding out the closest thing to exact change. The acne-spotted teen behind the register barely opened her eyes wide enough to take his money.

"I got lucky. Good parents, better genes…that stuff, you know?" She turned to run a credit card through the chip reader. "Hard work matters more. I could've graduated sooner if I were more disciplined."

The cashier slumped against his register and refused to touch what she'd bought, so Chelsea bagged the food herself. Dave had shoved his cans into his cart, barely bothering with bags.

"Look, I'm not a college guy—barely got my GED, but who gives a damn if you took it a little easy? You earned a break, as far as I see it, and you have every right to be proud. No need to pretend to be bashful."

"A piece of paper's only worth so much, Dave. Something tells me I'm not the only one with a gift around here." She left the conversation at that, turning to finish paying.

Dave swept out, unnerved. He'd spent his life looking right through people, seeing what they hid in the shadowy corners of their minds, and he couldn't shake the feeling that someone had finally done the same to him.

Chapter 6

"Hello there. What can I do you for?" Jack said to the man on his porch. The stranger looked to be about his age. He had a thick jaw, set hard, as if made from concrete, and hair of roughly the same color. Despite the age and stress having set into his face, he held himself with a severe rigor. A man's man, as Jack's pop would've said, with the kind of stubble you only see on people too busy working hard to spend their days preening and worrying about the stripes on their suits.

"Hello, Mr. Valenti. My name is Special Agent Theodore Jotun, I'm with the FBI." He opened his wallet to flash his ID. "We've been investigating a serial killing and need to ask if you've seen anything. You may have heard of the killer. Tabloids call him the Ghost." The agent cracked the slightest smile. "Not a name the Bureau supports, but we're more concerned with actions than words. May I come in?"

Jack nodded and opened the door, visibly paler. Jotun counted on one thing above all else: the fact that people didn't say no to him. He'd walked into countless homes without a warrant or a decent reason because the tenants were afraid of refusing an FBI agent—and he'd charmed his way into more than a few others by profiling them beforehand. Easy to know what people want to hear when you've parsed their social media and pulled their public records.

"Honey," Jack called, "we've got an FBI agent here lookin' to talk to us." To Theo, he offered the basic courtesies. "Would you like something to drink? Water, coffee? We just put a pot on. Bathroom's down the hall here if you need it."

He gave the warmest smile he could. "Coffee sounds great, thanks."

Theo's eyes scanned the house as they entered. *Quaint, almost. Simple people with simple tastes. Art painted by…ugh, by the lady of the house.* Self-aggrandizement didn't apply to Theo, of course, but for an ordinary person, showing off like this seemed tacky. The paintings were basic art class material at that. Flowers. A horse. A candle flickering beneath a starless sky, sur- rounded by creeping shadows, as it waited to be snuffed out. His gaze lingered. *Actually, I like that one.*

They made their way to the dining room. Theo sat where Chelsea usually did, and he knew she usually sat there, because her Facebook feed was set to public, giving him access to the entirety of her life in this dull residence. Jack plopped down at his right as Pauline brought over coffee, cream, and sugar. He thanked her and took a swig of his drink. Black, of course.

He liked it harsh and strong. Good things are supposed to hurt.

"Thank you for taking the time to speak with me." He looked between them, making extra eye contact with Mrs. Val- enti, because a woman like her would respond most favorably to strong acts of authority. "There's been a serial killer targeting young women across several states, and we believe he may be in the area. Have you seen anyone unusual around lately?"

"Oh my," Pauline gasped, eyes already watering. "You think he's targeting Chelsea?" Her shaking hands wrapped around her mug. Agent Jotun didn't react, because they'd know he consciously suppressed a reaction, which would make them think he suspected she was next.

Of course, she IS next. They don't need to know that. Not yet. But gods demand sacrifice, and mine, in particular, must be appeased.

Jotun shook his head. "We don't know who. So far, his vic- tims have all been slightly overweight, with dark hair and light eyes, usually small noses, about five-three in stature."

"Hey," Jack growled, "you watch yourself when you talk about my daughter."

Holding his hands up apologetically, he backpedaled, as he knew he would. "I'm sorry, Mr. Valenti, I didn't mean to offend. I'm just doing my job. I assume, then, she matches that description?"

Eyes flitting to his mug, Jack eased back in his chair, arms crossed. "Maybe a bit."

"Then, it's possible—not definite, but possible—that she is in danger, which is exactly why I need your cooperation. So far, the killer has introduced himself to the victim or the victim's family prior to taking anyone's lives. Has Chelsea mentioned any new friends, people who arrived in town recently?"

Both parents shook their heads.

"Do you know if she has any close friends, people she may try to get in contact with if she is in trouble? Sometimes people, especially young people, tell their friends things before telling their parents, to avoid worrying them."

Pauline elaborated on Chelsea's tight-knit group of friends, giving Jotun the women's full names, but lamented not having their numbers. Jack added that he couldn't think of any other significant people she had mentioned, but that she was always the quiet type.

"That's fine, this has been very helpful. You're sure that nothing strange has happened lately? No odd cars outside, no new neighbors? Nothing mentioned over a pool party, during a carpool?"

"Nothin'," Jack said. "No one's said a thing."

"Wait!" Pauline raised a finger. "A bartender. She didn't— our Chelsea's never shown much interest in men, but she did mention him. I think she ran into him at the store."

This wasn't according to plan. They weren't supposed to mention anyone. Those who did usually pointed a finger at a boyfriend they didn't like. Or girlfriend. Or whatever. But a bartender?

His eyes widened. Harmony. The video she saw.

"This bartender—do you know where he works, what he looks like?"

Pauline nodded, pulling out her phone from her pocket, opening a picture clearly shot by Chelsea. The angle was terrible, the lighting worse, but it showed all he needed. The Vessel. He really did work here. With careful planning, the Order could swoop them both up in one late-night abduction. A sacrifice to usher in their god's arrival, not merely slake its hunger.

Jotun finished his coffee and smiled. "Then I suppose that's all." He grinned. "You've both been enormously helpful."

Chapter 7

Chelsea arrived home with thoughts of Dave on her mind, her arms full of groceries, and a growling stomach. "Mom?" Her voice fell on a still house. "Dad?"

The car sat in the driveway, and it wouldn't have surprised her if they'd stepped over to a neighbor's. Her parents had grown pretty social in the years since she left for college, no doubt trying to overcome empty nest syndrome, or maybe celebrating their newfound freedom. Chelsea was never sure which, but always suspected one or the other. Usually, the other.

She set the groceries down on the floor in the hall so she could look at the mail. Being a child of the information age, she didn't get much print mail; what little she did she had sent to her parents' house, knowing they would call to tell her about it anyway. Her rule, one held by most people who'd grown up on the internet, was that if you had something to say to her, a text or email was generally the best way to ensure she got the message. Virtually, she could assure a prompt response. By snail mail, it'd take an act of God for her to write back soon.

To her surprise, a letter sat there, addressed to her: a normal white envelope, handwritten address for the sender, nothing written for the return. No stamp either, so whoever delivered it did so by hand, placing it atop a Shoprite coupon periodical and a Victoria's Secret catalog, where she couldn't miss it. Chelsea turned it over, scrutinizing the mysterious white rectangle, but other than the neat printing on the front (done with what looked like a blue-ink ballpoint pen, too general for more information), there didn't seem to be any discerning marks. It had even been sealed carefully, not a single crease or bump made in the adhesive as the sender pressed down.

"Who the hell would write me a letter?" she mumbled, pulling the envelope open. The letter itself was a single sheet of white, unlined paper. With the same print, the words, *Tuesday, January thirteenth, 7:13 PM* were written, seeming to shimmer.

Chelsea started to question the words—that was a little under a week away—when she recalled the details from 'The Ghost' news coverage.

First, he kills the victim's family.
Then, he sends her a note, saying when she'll disappear.
When that time comes, she does.

But this had to be a prank. *Why would anyone target me? He hasn't struck in months.*

She kept telling herself this. The words played on loop in her head as she walked into the kitchen. Though her eyes surveyed the scene, Chelsea argued with herself, figuring she was confused, dreaming, hallucinating, something, *anything.*

Shaking, her hands unconsciously covered her mouth, as if her body knew she wanted to scream before her brain encountered the stimulus that provoked it.

Sitting in their usual chairs, Pauline and Jack Valenti looked like they were chatting and waiting for their daughter to return home, except Jack's throat had been sliced open and Pauline had three bullets in her chest. The bodies had been propped to give the illusion of a casual evening. Blood coated their outfits, the table, and the floor around them. Red streaks ran along the wood where the bodies had been dragged.

Wrapped presents sat in the center of the table. Above, a banner read, "Happy birthday!"

They didn't move. This might still be a terrible, out-of-character prank, but that likelihood grew smaller by the second. She walked forward, ignoring the blood staining her shoes, intent on shaking her parents, but then she realized she could see into her mother's body. The wounds were real, and they were deep.

"Mom, no, no, no, no." She approached the body. Grabbing her mother's wrist, Chelsea tried to take a pulse but couldn't find one. She couldn't find one in the neck either. A quick calculation of the angle and wound size told her one bullet hit a lung while another hit the heart. No hope of surviving the barrage. Her lips trembled. Chelsea suppressed tears, resting her head on her mother's cold, cold thigh.

Her dad would've bled out in seconds, and probably died first. No way that bear would've heard his wife get shot and not immediately destroy the attacker. Peaceful or otherwise, you don't hurt a man's family without him reacting in kind.

Sinking back into the cool, analytical sanctuary of her mind, she tried to piece together what happened. Though no forensics expert, she reasoned, based on the lack of forced entry and a faint arterial spray on the far wall, that whoever did this was invited in. Probably introduced himself under false pretenses. Jack would've sat down, invited him to coffee and a snack, as was his nature, not realizing the danger until he was already dying. A splash pattern indicated he likely tried to stand in his last moments but fell.

A faltering in the otherwise clean wound told her the killer used his left hand. The crimson spray on the wall behind her mother, and the two black holes, indicated she'd stood, understandably shocked and probably about to scream, when the killer opened fire. It was likely a silenced gun, or the neighbors would've reported something. Pauline looked like she fell back into the chair, gasping, trying to catch breath with one ruined lung and another that was filling with blood. If she was lucky, the shock would've caused her to black out; if not, her last moments would've been spent drowning on dry land. One bullet was still in the body.

All she wanted to do was curl up in her treehouse and be a child again. There was innocence in her youthful naiveté that she hadn't been able to understand or appreciate until it was gone. She'd spent so much time there, lost in her own world of books and make-believe where nothing could hurt her. Chelsea never made many friends. Her relationships felt fleeting and shallow, even then. She spent her early years trying to fill a void in her heart with imagination and storytelling. Later, she'd turned to food. Neither worked.

Her unraveling mind wondered if going there might turn the clock back, maybe not to childhood but long enough for her to scream *RUN* and watch her parents get away.

Shaking her head, she chided herself. *Don't get emotional.* Chelsea had made a career out of numbing herself to pain, and this was another task to be overcome, for now. There'd be time to cry later. There'd be time for her to punch mirrors and scream "Why me?" like they do in movies. There'd be a time for her to run away, change her name, cut her hair, and turn into someone else, into someone even her few friends wouldn't recognize. This was not that time.

Taking out her phone, Chelsea dialed 9-1-1.

"9-1-1, what's your emergency?"

Keeping her voice as steady as she could, Chelsea told the operator the blunt truth. "My parents are dead." Her timber was still shaky and faint, but so far so good.

"Dead? Are you sure, ma'am? Can you tell me your name please?" Though operators were trained to be calm, this one sounded notably perturbed. Probably new to the job.

"Chelsea. Valenti. I'm sure. Please send officers to sixty-three, Pendleton Avenue, White Plains."

"Sixty-three, Pendleton Avenue, White Plains. Is that right?"

The shaking was fading, replaced by her normal cool dissociation. "Yes."

"Can you tell me what's happening?"

Staring at the pool of blood, she relayed the key information. "I was at the store. I came home. They…they were here. My mom's been shot. Dad…someone slit his throat."

"The police are on their way. Stay with me, okay, Chelsea?"

"Okay." She stared at the tiled wall behind the toaster as intently as she could, wondering if companies would still hire her after this. It'd be in the papers for sure. No one likes hiring damaged goods. There'd probably be years of therapy, assuming a therapist could break down her walls at all.

"Is there anyone else there with you?"

"No." Her responses came slow but automatic, unthinking, distant.

"I want you to check for a pulse, okay, Chelsea?"

"I have." She swallowed. "They're dead."

"If you aren't sure, I can walk you through the steps."

"I know how to check a pulse."

"What you do is place your index and middle fingers against the person's—"

Chelsea hung up. Picking up the killer's letter from the floor, she folded both it and the envelope, reaching for her purse to tuck them away for future scrutiny. Then, reasoning the police might search her bag, she tucked the paper into her bra. Police may be thorough, but they don't strip search people who've found their parents murdered.

Someone had killed her parents, and now she would be next, whether the police helped or not—but if she brought it to their attention, the note would be confiscated as evidence. In her hands, she could analyze it, try to figure out the handwriting pattern, maybe profile the killer, but not if the cops got involved. Plus, they'd want her in custody, to keep her in witness protection, something. According to past victims, that would leave her vulnerable. He'd killed seven people in 'protective' custody already. They clearly weren't able to stop him.

Grabbing the groceries, she returned to the kitchen, eyes deftly avoiding the blood bath nearby. She put extreme attention into putting the food away, ensuring it was ordered and neatly placed on their respective shelves. The stuff in the refrigerator would likely go bad if nobody hung around to eat it, but there was no sense in leaving it on the counter.

The front door opened, and a series of footfalls came through the front rooms. "Chelsea, are you alright? This is Officer…" A uniformed man stepped into the kitchen, followed by his partner, trailing off as he saw the carnage. Then he spied Chelsea. "Jesus Christ, Mike, get her out of here." His voice was a decibel above a mumble.

Mike stepped over, hand at her back. "Let's step outside. You don't need to see this."

Nodding, Chelsea let him lead her toward the door and take her outside, saying nothing. That night seemed darker than those before it, and she couldn't help but wonder what vicious eyes hid in the shadows.

Chapter 8

The Grand Master smiled as his masses left their meeting hall, both out of his usual adoration of their support and out of excitement for how well his two goals were going. The newest sacrifice's family had been dispatched with ease. Soon he would step in to take her back to their compound, where he'd slowly take her life. She'd call the police, report a murder, go into protective custody, and his followers would hack into the precinct database to find her location. They'd scramble LEO feeds while he blocked things at the federal level. It would take the FBI too long to get involved. She'd be dead by the time his fellow agents knew she'd been a target.

Now, in perfect synchronicity, she and the Vessel were in the same area, and they even knew each other. They could take both away in the dead of night, and their god would be wreaking havoc upon the earth by this time next week.

"Grand Master," Harmony said, startling him from his thoughts, "may I ask you something?"

They were alone now, as they always seemed to be when she spoke to him.

"Certainly. What is it?" He raised an eyebrow.

"When we find the Vessel and merge him with the Incarnate, bringing Nyoru to our world, what then?" She cocked her head.

"What do you mean?"

"Well, aside from a life without pain, what will we do? Our god will not need our help at that point. Nyoru may grant us peace and hope, but what do we do after if there's no need for the Order? I can't imagine the Saint of Glorious Pain will need servants once the world learns of its existence."

It was a fair enough question—one that no one else had asked, and it left him stumped. He'd never given thought to that. He'd be immortal, or nearly so, once he became Nyoru, and had no considerations for his loyal flock.

"That," he said, "will be up to he Saint, who will direct us when the time comes." The answer was sufficiently vague and thus sounded wise and mystical. To him, at least.

"Is that why we sacrifice people? Does their pain grant us a promise of future pleasure?"

"Of course."

"Then why do all the sacrifices look the same? Why are our members not counted as sacrifices, even when they suffer and die for our Saint?"

His lips pressed into a thin line. He tried not to think of the photo he'd since stashed in a drawer, so he didn't have to see it sitting on his desk.

"*The Black Tome* is specific, and it is the word of our god. I don't question it. You shouldn't either." Theo maintained eye contact, straightening his back to command as much authority as he could.

Harmony knew things were bad. Letting the Vessel elude their grasp had been bad, but there was more at play, more trouble bubbling away beneath the surface. The last few weeks had been tumultuous at best, his concentration, his control, his composure all slipping, slipping, sinking away like spilled blood oozing from a slit wrist to circle its way down the bathtub drain.

"Thank you, Grand Master. That was very helpful." She slipped from the room.

Theo drew a picture of Chelsea from his pocket. Harmony was right about one thing: they all looked the same. Like one woman who'd died years ago, as the first sacrifice, unintentional though it may have been.

Staring at the picture, he sighed, shaking his head at his memories. Though he stared at Chelsea's image, he didn't speak to her. "It's a pity you won't see my ascension. I know you would love to see me become a god, but you've suffered enough."

Part Two: Desolate Roads

Chapter 9

Chelsea's 'going away party' took place at Mickey's the next day, like any other time they might've gone out for a drink, except Chelsea spoke even less than usual, her eyes fixated on the rim of her drink. Her parents' wills had left everything to a trust. She'd worry about the money later. Survival came first.

She had, of course, lied when they asked why she was leaving town. "A job offer," she'd said, "in California."

"Are you sure you're alright?" Theresa said, laying a hand over her wrist. Perceptive as ever, the yogi was easily able to figure out that tonight's lack of communication was not from being lost in thought, as it usually was.

Nodding, she finished the rest of her glass and forced a smile. *Don't think about it. Don't think about it. If you start thinking about why you're leaving, you'll cry and they'll know something's wrong, so focus on the stupid Coke and the way it burns your throat because the pain will take your mind off it.*

Eyebrows arched, Jordan cut in. "Seriously, we're gonna be your friends anyway, so don't act like you have to go apologizing. We get it."

Theresa added, "I'm surprised you want to have our last get-together here, though."

Last get-together. Knowing how the Ghost cases usually progressed, she figured that night could be the last time she got to sit down and enjoy someone else's company. Her own little *Last Supper*, comprised of watered down non-alcoholic drinks and stale bar pretzels.

Giving the sincerest smile she could, Chelsea looked each of her friends in the eye, one by one. "Thanks, guys. I appreciate it. Be right back, okay?" She slid out from the seat before anyone could object and approached the bar.

Upon first arriving, they'd ordered drinks from one of the veteran bartenders, a man in his early thirties who still acted like he was in his twenties called Joe Michaels. He had been nice enough to offer the first round for free, or perhaps thought he was smooth enough to be able to take one of them home at the end of the night. Now, she saw Dave had returned, looking as disinterested as ever as he cleaned glasses.

"Virgin daiquiri. Keep the change." She held out a twenty-dollar bill.

Dave looked her over. "No change on a twenty? You sure? I know you college girls are broke."

"Life's too short to be cheap about a tip." Chelsea tried not to think about why she was so certain she wouldn't need her money anymore. "Besides, you're leaving town soon, right? You probably need cash for the road." A twinge of envy crept into her voice. She'd be hitting the road soon, too, and it'd be nice to have a companion, but she couldn't impose that kind of risk on some unsuspecting stranger.

Her strained voice caught Dave's attention. He stopped what he was doing to look up, locking eyes with her. For an instant, she felt entranced by his gaze, world blurring blue at the edges. The azure depths held answers to questions she dared not ask. Then the spell was broken, as suddenly as it had started, with no indication as to what had happened, but she recognized that tug. He'd done the same thing to her the other night over the stupid peanut.

"Aw, hell." His eyes darted around the bar.

"What?" Chelsea stared. He knew something, just refused to let on, and worse, she didn't have half a clue to what.

"It's…It's nothing. I just…" Grimacing, he looked back

down at the glasses, picking up a rag to clean and then dropping it again.

Now curious, she leaned over the bar. "You're not good at keeping secrets." He refused, so she pressed on. "What, you want to ask me out?" *Imagine the irony: someone asks me on a date just as I'm about to...*She tried not to entertain that line of thought.

Dave shut his eyes, tilting his head down toward the counter. "I can't stand to see innocent people get hurt. I...have a gift. So, I know what happened to you last night." He leaned forward, bracing his elbows against the bar. "You have my most sincere condolences. Really, you do. I know what it's like to lose your parents. Here, take all the drinks you want, on the house. It's the least I can do." Putting her daiquiri and her twenty on the counter, he added, "I need to check on something."

He walked into the back before she could respond.

WHAT THE HELL? Her parents' blood had barely cooled on the kitchen floor, yet somehow, this random bartender knew the details of what happened—and the cops had made damn sure none of it wound up in the paper.

Part of her was angry, confused, and slightly violated at the idea that a complete stranger could know something so personal, but most of her was happy to have another puzzle to solve. It gave her an extended window of time in which she wouldn't have to feel anything, especially with a riddle like this: no clues, no one to ask for help, and defiance of reason. She'd been with him at the grocery store when her parents were murdered, so how did he know? He couldn't have been the killer. He couldn't have been. But how else would he know all that?

There was no logical reason for Dave to know such details, but ultimately, everything must have a reason, and she resolved to find it. As she walked back to her seat, the need to understand the enigmatic man she'd just spoken to replaced all thought of wanting to protect herself or her identity.

And on the plus side, he did say he was leaving town.

"You took your sweet time." Jordan smirked, glancing at

the bar, the same way Chelsea's dad used to smirk about playing jokes on his wife. "Dave chatting you up?"

Figuring it would be best to leave out any and all significant association, she shook her head. "Just making sure my tab is paid off."

"We would've taken care of that for you!" Teresa smiled. "But it's good of you to make sure the bill is paid before you leave."

Especially because I won't be coming back. But my parents always said to pay your dues. Square up before you duck out. Don't leave anything unfinished, or it'll come find you later. It's the whole reason she arranged this night out. If she vanished, they'd come looking. They'd be at risk. She couldn't allow that.

"So, what are we up to next? Bowling, bingo?" Jordan joked sarcastically. Asking Jordan to get her sister involved wasn't an option. Even the FBI had failed to stop the Ghost so far, and Talia had only joined the Bureau a few years ago. She didn't have the pull to get anything serious done—assuming they could do anything.

Across the room, Dave seemed to be in an argument with the manager, Danielle. Unlike most such standoffs, it seemed pretty quiet and well-contained. If anything, Danielle seemed to be pleading with him, desperate about something, but Dave shook his head and walked out the front door. A heavy-looking bag hung from his left hand.

He'd just quit. Why the urgency? And right after their conversation?

"I really should go pack. I'm sorry but my…My parents, they would want me home, to…" She drifted off quickly, eyes stinging, so she shook her head. *Focus, damn it, focus, focus! Don't get emotional. Not now. Please, not now.* Despite her friends' disappointment, Chelsea gave them all quick hugs.

"Thanks again, everyone. I'll email, or text you, or, you know, whatever I can do."

She felt bad about leaving so abruptly, but Dave was leaving even more swiftly, and if she didn't catch him soon, she might not catch him at all. Weaving through the crowd, she managed to get to the door, exiting out into the parking lot.

Across the lamplight asphalt, Dave's lanky figure was approaching a run-down, indiscriminate four-door car. Glad she'd worn flats, Chelsea did her best to jog across the lot, one hand clutched around her purse and the other trying to stop her breasts bouncing too much. Some things don't change regardless of the situation, and for Chelsea, one of those was the embarrassment that came from trying to run.

"Dave." She slowed, still halfway across the lot but now half-walking, half-stumbling. Since she rarely ran, she had no stamina, and he was almost to the driver's side door.

Casting a frantic glance around the street, he crossed the lot to meet her.

"What are you doing?" he hissed, harsh and low through clenched teeth.

"Let me come with you, please." Out of breath, she did her best to, as Theresa would describe, focus her breathing, and slow down her obnoxious gasping.

"No, that is completely out of the question. If you need help, if you want protection, go to the cops. Go to the FBI. Go to Sports Authority and buy yourself a gun. I don't know, you seem like a smart girl. I'm sure you'll think of something, but you're not coming with me." He turned to walk back to his car.

"I can pay you if that's the problem. I'm not sure how you know about my parents, but I'm pretty sure you didn't kill them, and if you did, well, right now, I'm probably going to die anyway." His posture broke a little, stone façade crumbling. "You play cold and aloof, but we both know this loner act is to keep people from getting hurt. I majored in psych, remember? I know when people are running from something."

Dave looked off at the empty road leading out of town. "Like I said, cops, FBI, Sports Authority. Hotwire a car and set out for Nevada. Break into an abandoned house and live out of the basement. If you're that desperate, rob a convenience store and wait for the cops to throw you in jail. I'm sure the guy can't get you there."

"Who cares what you're hiding? If it's dangerous, there's no way it's more dangerous than what's going to happen to me."

"You'd be surprised," he scoffed.

"Look, I can pay you a lot. Fifty thousand, at least."

"Money isn't the problem! And even if it was, I wouldn't accept it. Jesus, I wouldn't make you pay me to keep you alive."

"Then why won't you help me?" Chelsea's voice shot up an octave, forcing her to realize maybe this wasn't all about the puzzle. Either way, she lowered her voice and went back to her analytical stance. "I am begging you, get me out of here. You said you don't want to see innocent people get hurt, so why won't you help?"

Dropping his voice to match, Dave whispered back, giving a furtive glance around: "Because I skip town a lot, okay? I change names, burn my identity. Can't remember the time I was one person for more than a few months. I am not 'Dave Helmholtz.'"

"Oh, like I don't already know that." Chelsea scowled. He recoiled, shocked, so she continued, "You show up out of nowhere, suddenly working at this bar that hasn't had new staff since W. Bush was in office, barely remembering to respond to your own fake name half the time, then trying to pass it off like you didn't hear because the bar's kinda loud sometimes." She crossed her arms over her chest. "Fake your identity if you want, but you suck at hiding it."

His jaw hung slack for a moment, then tightened with anger. "You think you'll get a ride out of town by insulting me? What's next, you blackmail me, threaten to post what you said online, blow my cover and all that?"

"No." Chelsea shook her head. "I wouldn't. Ever. But I can see you actually *like* talking to me. Not that you like me, just that you know I see you for who you really are. And like you said, you've been on the run a *long* time. I can see that, too. So, one day, you're going to think of me again, and you're going to find my obituary, and you'll know you let the only person to see you for who you really are die. When that happens, it's not going to matter who you're running from, because my death will kill you."

They locked eyes for a moment, and again Chelsea felt that hypnotic tug, like the universe was a tube with him at one end and her at the other, and there was nowhere for their energy to go except in or out of their bodies. When he broke the trance and the silence a moment later, he said, "Go home and pack a bag. Necessities only. When you're done, call this number," he took a pencil from his pocket and scribbled on the back of a discarded receipt, "and we will arrange a remote pickup. You have to leave your car at your house, or someone will get suspicious and report a derelict vehicle, but I can't go to your house in case it's being watched. You have until eleven pm to do this or I will assume you're dead, abducted, or in police custody, and will leave without you. Understand?"

She nodded. "Understood." They separated, and once behind the wheel of her car, she noted that this gave her under an hour and a half to get home and get ready.

Watching Dave pull away, Chelsea felt a flutter of hope's wings beating against the sorrow raging inside her. Beyond that, she knew the puzzle of this man was beginning to reveal itself.

Maybe I can't see the center of the puzzle, but the edges are coming together.

Chapter 10

Special Agent Theodore Jotun walked through the hallways of the New York FBI headquarters, eyes glancing fervently from one coworker to the next. As per usual, the office was abuzz with chatter, none of it useful. Conversations ranged from the broken coffee machine to the graffiti in the second stall in the men's room, from getting a flat while investigating a shooting in Albany to spending the coming week-long vacation in Atlantic City. He'd been with the Bureau long enough to know that it wasn't nearly as glamorous as he thought it would be when he first joined.

Most would say it was still a great place to work, that updates in law enforcement technology, redesigned weapons, and more strategic investigation procedures made being an FBI agent safer than it had ever been before. Others would point out that arrest rates had increased in the last five years, rising on a steady incline as if to indicate that the world was, in fact, improving.

Whether or not the moral fiber of the world was stronger or growing more corrupt was not something that can be measured with facts and figures. Morality was an abstraction, fully comprehendible only by those who were willing to abandon rationality in favor of more profound ideas—this was something he reminded his followers daily.

Harmony, in particular, seemed inclined to grasp the abstract in a manner both quicker and more impressive than that which he expected from somebody who went to community college to major in a social science, but he had to concede that it might be her constant immersion in the ebb and flow of the mundane that left her so open to the idea of something greater than herself. Nothing makes a person crave the irrational like a too rational life.

For the time being, he had to focus on the task at hand, which was delivering the latest report on the Hudson Hounds, a group theorized to be an evolved street gang that stretched out over several cities, primarily those in southern New York and northern New Jersey, and seemed to be growing. The director would not be happy to know they still had no tangible evidence that could lead to incriminating any of those involved, but at the very least, they now had enough evidence to officially classify the group as a gang, right up there with the Latin Kings and Juggalos. He wouldn't have bothered to tell her this if his partner, Agent Talia Garcia, weren't so damn persistent. Her closure rate was twice his, a fact he justified by saying his cases were harder.

The director's office was set back a way from the main work room, an architectural and strategic maneuver that would allow the other agents to protect those in command positions should anyone be stupid enough to walk into an FBI headquarters and open fire, but still smart enough to sneak a gun pass the metal detectors. He paused briefly at Agent Garcia's desk, who was rumored to have a younger sister, though she never discussed her personal life. As always, Agent Garcia had her head buried in another file and glanced up only long enough to confirm that she'd received a copy. On the off chance the director wanted a briefing, they would need to give the appearance of solidarity, an illusion that would not fool the rest of the agents given their strained work history.

Though it looked like she wanted to ask him something, he walked off, pointedly ignoring any potential query. He made his way down the command hall, one with linoleum floors and bland, off-white walls, like the rest of the building. Near-dead halogen bulbs hung overhead, reminding him of how far the law enforcement budget had fallen over the recent years, a faltering some of his more boisterous coworkers attributed to a combination of ineffective war policy and "Obama," though his name was thrown around in relation to anything going wrong, including the fact that nobody had fixed the coffee machine.

Giving three hard knocks to the door labeled "Director Luisa D'Armillo," Agent Jotun stepped inside. Some would balk at the idea of walking into a superior's office without waiting for confirmation that one could do so, but the door only led into a small waiting room, one that, on this day, only held her secretary. The secretary glanced up over the rim of his frameless glasses, his brown eyes seeming more like the bark of a dead tree than they ever had before.

"I'm afraid the director is in a meeting right now. You'll have to come back later," he said with all the interest of an atheist at Sunday Mass.

"The director specifically asked to meet with me, so I'll wait here."

The overweight secretary shifted, causing the mechanisms of his chair to squeak in protest. Objects at rest tend to stay at rest for a reason, such as not having to adjust to a heaving mass of human flesh suddenly shifting its momentum.

"You know, my job is to make sure this office runs smoothly, so I'm supposed to tell people what to do while they are here." He sneered.

"Maybe so, but I don't have to listen."

Agent Jotun turned his eyes to the file, officially marked *File AB-183-X33,* casually referred to as "File X33" or, according to Agent Garcia, "The next great domestic threat to the American way." In the past year alone, there had been forty-seven abductions or killings that were suspected to have been perpetrated by the Hudson Hounds.

Unlike most gangs, this one was smarter and subtler; there were no drive-bys, no street dealings, no operating out of ramshackle houses at the end of dead-end streets in the poorer parts of towns. They'd managed to avoid police detection for years, and even the Bureau had no knowledge of when exactly they had first come into existence. The only reason a file on this group even existed was because one of their former members had turned whistleblower on them, saying that he was recruited to help manufacture drugs—but the names he gave turned up nothing in the Bureau's systems, and the address he gave as to their "headquarters" was an abandoned house that hadn't been lived in for years. A complete forensic sweep revealed nothing, except for one fingerprint that turned out to belong to the previous owner, a woman who died years ago. Not that they were an actual gang—there had been enough clues to give the illusion of one.

The door to the director's office opened. "Agent Jotun, step inside please."

"The director will see you now," Tommy said.

Agent Jotun and Director D'Armillo both looked at him, then wordlessly entered, shutting the door. Her office was plainly furnished with a large touchscreen wirelessly linked to her computer and several chairs. Aside from a bookshelf with a half-dead cactus and the most recent books on investigative techniques and management exercises, there was little else in the room.

"Where do we stand on the Hounds investigation?" she said, her hazel eyes radiating like two colored floodlights. Some said she rose to her position solely on the intensity of her probing gaze.

Clearing his throat, the agent said, "We are...making some headway. Some. We've gathered enough witness testimony to add them to the list of street gangs."

She narrowed her eyes at him.

"But," he continued, "I think we have a lead. See, a man and woman in Black Haven, over in Jersey, reported their middle child went missing. He'd been acting suspicious over the past few weeks and disappeared without warning; we think, based on the gang's MO, that he was contacted and recruited."

Glaring at him, the director said, "A couple reports a child acting weird and then running off, and you call that a lead on your case...How, exactly?"

He knew it wasn't a real lead but played his part. "I-I'm sorry, director?"

"I mean, by what loose standards do you define a lead? What you have, Agent Jotun, is so circumstantial a judge would laugh if you used that to get a search warrant."

He adjusted his collar. "Sorry, ma'am, but the parents did send us his computer, said we could go through it, and a man described as 'suspicious with unusual tattoos' came looking for him the day before."

"In the future, start with that."

"Understood."

Rubbing her temple, she sat down behind her desk, clicking around on her computer. She hadn't invited him to sit so he remained standing until she reached down and pulled out a remote. Clicking the power button a few times, she hissed under her breath and rapped it against her desk before pressing the button again. The TV turned on to display a series of red dots along a map of the US.

"Based on your report, this is an aerial view of all the Hounds related deaths in the last few months. Though based out of New York"—she indicated with a laser pointer—"you show the crimes are spreading to small towns."

"Yes, I believe they're scouting to take over local business-es, much like the mafia did in previous decades. They may be-lieve themselves to be a bit, eh, old world." Another look from the director had him backpedaling. "Not that there's anything wrong with old world Italians!"

This time, she smiled. "I'm not going to chew you out over that one, Theo. My dad would've had you running for your life, but not me."

He idly wondered what a lone man would do when faced with the full power of his followers, but he was obviously not going to voice that aloud.

"We need leads, damn it," she sighed.

"We always need leads."

"If this hits the internet, we're screwed. What do you think most people will do when they realize this group is an actual threat and they had to hear about it from some jackass with a blog since we can't handle it?"

"They…will…" He trailed off. Agent Jotun was never sure what to say in these situations. When he was leading the conversation, he was fine, but playing subordinate drove him crazy.

"They will destroy us, Theo. Find us some leads before the public finds a reason to put our heads on goddamn stakes."

"Understood, ma'am," he said. "I'll go find some leads, right now."

Nodding to him, she clicked the TV off as he left, ignoring Tommy as he made his way to Agent Garcia, back in the main room.

"What'd she want?" his partner asked.

He shrugged. "What everyone wants. Answers."

Chapter 11

"You know...this silence after, this...nothingness. It's almost as bad as finding them." Chelsea looked over at Dave from the passenger's seat, but he didn't respond.

Turning, she locked her eyes on the waning moon. In accordance with Dave's plan, she had gone home, packed a bag, reached out to him, and arranged to leave White Plains as soon as possible. He'd instructed her to walk a few blocks—a few nerve-racking, poorly lit, shadow strewn blocks, during which time she kept one eye constantly glancing back over her shoulder—to a nearby bus station. Once there, she'd ridden one of the few late buses over to the town library, and from there she walked to a convenience store set a little off the main road, where there wouldn't be many people. Waiting across the street, Chelsea tried not to let her heart leap through her throat and out her mouth every time somebody walked by, but there weren't many people out. Dave picked her up, as he said he would, and they began making their way out of town.

Now, with nothing but her silent companion and the open road, all attempts at conversation falling flat, she had nothing with which to distract herself. The puzzle beside her would offer her no pieces, the image remaining obscure; the full moon, great as it was, cast no light on the darkness she was suffering through, offered her no solace. The Pennsylvanian woods, seeming treacherous at night as the trees twisted and contorted, mocked her.

Her whisper, though quiet and to herself, prompted Dave

to speak for the first time in almost an hour. "You should get some rest."

Chelsea shook her head. "You said we'll be there soon, right? I'll sleep once we get there. I don't really sleep in cars."

"Still…" He glanced around, checking his blind spots, before merging into the right lane. "People need extra sleep during…times of stress."

"If I shut my eyes, I'll see it again. I need distractions, not sleep."

Again, he was silent. They drove on for a few minutes before he took an exit ramp. She didn't see what number.

"We all have to face what we deal with, one way or another. Pain can be toxic. A little bit will stress you out, and a lot of it can kill you, sure as any disease, injury, or poison."

"So, what? You think I should face it all, try to deal with it? How exactly do you get over your parents dying?" she snapped, glaring at him.

The car made a left turn onto a dirt road. "You don't." He sounded cold and distant.

Rubbing the bridge of her nose, she said, "I'm sorry. You didn't…That was crappy of me. Here you are saving my life, and…"

"You're stressed, traumatized, tired, probably hungry. Don't worry about it."

They pulled up outside a small cabin-like structure, the door locked, windows boarded shut from the outside.

"Didn't you say you lost your parents?" The moonlight illuminated the clearing and the inside of the car—except for Dave. He appeared to have a protective cloak of darkness thrown around his shoulders.

"Come on, we should get inside. You really do need rest, and we shouldn't stay here for more than a day or two." Stepping out of the car, he walked around to the back seat, picking up their bags. He was halfway to the cabin itself, a wood building with ivy growing along the side and roof partially covered in moss before she got out and caught up with him.

"Not for more than a day or two? You really think people will find us out here?"

Dave nudged the door open and stepped back. When nothing happened, he took a flashlight from his bag and aimed it around. There was only one room; it had a bed frame, a musty sofa, and a stone fireplace. Pressing a finger to his lips, he walked inside and scrutinized the area for a few minutes. Once satisfied, he said, "Possibly. I used this place once before but didn't have a better alternative. I won't be able to use it again."

Dave took a gas lantern out of his bag, turned it on, and set it on the floor in the center of the room. The cabin had a reddish hue to the floors and walls, making Chelsea think first of cedar, and then blood. She grimaced and shut her eyes for a moment, and when she opened them, Dave was gone.

She darted to the doorway and saw him rummaging through the trunk of a car. She let out a gasp and put her hand to her chest, feeling her heart thrum spasmodically. Stepping back in and putting her back to the wall, she repeated, *Focus your breathing...Focus your breathing...It's okay...He's still here.*

His footsteps came crunching across the ground outside. As he entered, she said, "You—"

Letting out the faintest gasp of surprise, Dave's head snapped around and he locked eyes with Chelsea. Again, his gaze held her immobile, this time as his eyes became reflective. She saw herself, hit with the sudden and distinct impression that her cat had been run over by a truck. This didn't make sense because she didn't have a cat, and even if she did, it wasn't around for a truck to crush, but still a wave of grief, loss, and anger swept through her and she felt as though a family pet, and indeed a close friend, had been taken from her life. She sank to the floor in tears, head in her hands, her rational mind screaming, *Get up, get up! What is your problem? You don't have a cat!*

But still, her cat was dead. Her imaginary, never-having-existed cat was splattered beneath someone's four-wheel-drive, and she was crying over its not-present body.

"Damn it, damn it, I'm so sorry." He dropped to the floor. "What did I hit you with? Look up, look at me. It's okay."

She shook her head, tears spattering along the hardwood beneath her, leaving dark impressions that shouldn't logically have been made, but something illogical had happened and now the cat Chelsea never had was really dead. "I don't, I don't..." She sobbed. "I don't like cats! Dave, *I don't even like cats!*"

"I know, just look at me, okay?"

"No, you don't understand!" Her heart clenched tight, breaking as it hammered against her ribcage. "Cats suck! But I...but I..."

"You miss the cat, I know. Chelsea." He put his hand under her chin and tilted her head upward. Following his lead, she looked at him through tear-stained vision and met his gaze. As before, she found herself locked in a trance, and this time his eyes seemed to glow a soft blue. The world tunneled to just him and her. A second later, there was no cat, again. No lost friend, no cat, no truck, and she was left with red eyes, confusion, and a detached memory of pain.

Now tearing up himself, Dave said, in a throaty, struggling-not-to-cry voice, "Better?" He wiped a bead as it rolled from his eye, but she swore it was a drop of blood.

She nodded, following the gesture with a shaky-voiced question. "What was that?"

"I...Remember when I said I knew about your parents, you being targeted?"

She nodded.

A sigh escaped him, as shuddering and tense as her voice had been. "I was born with a...special ability, I suppose. When I make eye contact with people, I can read their memories. If I choose, I can take the joy or pain out of them, or I can project that emotion I've stored onto other people. What you felt...A nine-year-old girl watched her cat die. Twelve years later—to the day—she's at the bar where you met me, celebrating her twenty-first birthday, still missing that cat like the day it died. I decided peace of mind was a good birthday gift.

"Before, you surprised me. Like I said, others are after me, too. When surprised, I sometimes can't control what I do, so I accidentally 'shot' you with a memory. I expected you to be by the lamp, but when you jumped out from the side...Anyway, sorry about that."

Nothing he said should've made sense. It was the type of nonsense you see spewing out of the mouths of those who need a double dose of lithium to make it through the day. Or those who go on spree killings.

But here she was, having witnessed what he was talking about firsthand. The trance, the tunnel-shaped world, the reflective eyes, none of it made a damn bit of sense. None of it conformed to anything she knew about the universe. But here it was, happening anyway.

Then, on a hunch, she thought back to her parents. She saw them sitting at the table, drenched in blood, the ruined birthday gifts; she remembered how it felt for her dad to wrap her up in his arms and squeeze so tight she thought she might die.

But there was no pain in her heart when she remembered her parents' lifeless eyes.

No anguish when she thought about how she'd never see them again.

All her pain disappeared. This time, that hollow in her chest felt welcoming. She didn't have to miss her parents. Neither pain nor pleasure. Just...being.

"You took more than the cat, didn't you?" she said, not knowing whether to be grateful or angry.

"I did. Yes. I didn't want to risk you freaking out all night."

Thinking back again, she saw the note and felt fear, violation, and anger. The echo of her friends saying goodbye and knowing it really was the last time she'd see them brought tears to her eyes.

"But not everything," she whispered, more to herself now.

"No. I figured…let you adapt to some of it. Like I said, too much pain can be toxic." Getting up, he retrieved a rolled-up air mattress and walked to the bed frame. Picking up a small motor, he began to inflate it. The device was noisy for something so small, the sound filling the cabin, prompting her to glance anxiously outside, but he didn't seem worried.

Chelsea decided the right emotion to settle on was reluctant gratitude. Her memories were hers, and she didn't like the idea of someone taking part of that away, even if all he took was the pain. But it did save her the trouble of having to keep up her defenses. Dad always told her there's no shame in turning to other people when you need help, and she definitely needed it now. She had to be a little grateful, too. Her emptiness didn't hurt. If anything, she welcomed it.

Being tracked by a serial killer wasn't an easy thing to deal with, but at least she could break it down more easily now. So long as she had contingency plans, analyzed for clues, factors, evidence, and related things, she wouldn't have to worry. The killer may have eluded police detection, but she was smart enough—she hoped—to stay ahead of him.

The death of her parents, though? That couldn't be broken down, it couldn't be overcome. They were gone, and there was no changing that. No fixing it. Once she got past losing her friends and the immediate shock of being almost killed, she would ask him for that pain back. Or before they parted ways. Whichever came first.

"You should get some sleep." He shut and locked the door. The bed had been made; he moved to the couch and lay down, sending a thin layer of dust into the air. "I can sleep with the light on if you want. I know some people are scared of the dark. If you don't, flip the switch when you're ready."

Twisting around, he pulled a thin blanket out of his bag and wrapped it around himself, burying his face against the back of the couch.

"You were going to say about your family…?" she couldn't help asking, and immediately hated doing so. He now carried the pain of losing *both* their parents.

Turning back, he stared at her for a second before saying, "My mother died when I was a boy. My dad…he had good intentions; went about raising me the wrong way, though. Thought getting physical would teach me how to be the man he wanted. I ran away when I was twelve. And that's enough about me." He rolled over. The silence of the cabin was stiffer, much more final than before.

Glancing down at her own bag, she debated changing, but Dave was right there. She turned to ask where she could change, then heard snoring coming from the couch. It wouldn't feel right changing in the open like that though. Chelsea wriggled under the covers before swapping her skirt for sweats. Eyeing her mysterious companion, she reached out and flicked the light off.

Chapter 12

Theo scrutinized the pile of papers on his desk. It was a hodgepodge of FBI cases, essays, personal documents, and religious texts. Of course, the Order's holy book sat in the left corner, on the side closer to him than his guests. This, a leather-bound book with no title, was the manuscript by which he ran his cult. It dictated the hierarchy of power within the organization, the rules which all members would follow, and the rituals, incantations, prayers, and stories of their god, Nyoru.

While some speculated that Theo wrote the book himself, he maintained that it had been passed down to him by his grandfather, who received it from an anthropologist, who received it from a blind man found staggering through the desert, his eyes having been gouged from his head. That man, the story went, was a lunatic, and no one believed the tome he passed on had any merit, and, in fact, the only reason it made it to Theo's grandfather was the fact that the anthropologist had forgotten it was in his possession. Allegedly, he had been under the impression Winston Jotun would throw it away, but it turned up beneath a shirt in his suitcase.

Theo's grandfather had taken good care of the book, making sure to keep the cover oiled so it wouldn't crack. When microfilm was developed, he made copies of every page; when copying technology reached a point that he could replicate the book easily, and at a low cost, he did so, making sure the book was preserved. After this, the old man began to bind the replicated pages, aiming to give them the same high-quality leather that the original had. He believed replicating the book would, as an act of worship, bestow the Saint's blessings, and he would know all there was to know about suffering and solace.

The day he completed the leather binding—and, in fact, at the exact instant he put the last stitch in place—his heart stopped. At the funeral, Theo heard a family friend say it was as if he died because he had no other purpose left to live for. Yet, the young man couldn't shake the feeling that something had kept him alive to finish what he started.

And now, over thirty years later, he still had it, in as close to mint condition as one can keep a book that is read almost every day. On more than one occasion, he wrote out the text of the book, copying the diagrams with as much exactitude as he could muster.

Resting his left hand on the book, which he and his followers had come to call *The Black Tome*, he opened the Hudson Hound file once again. He'd gone to great lengths to ensure there weren't leads on this case. Much like stonewalling the Ghost investigation, he needed to avoid any progress on the Hounds, because his Order occasionally needed new acolytes—or to silence those who discovered their real activities. These disappearances and deaths were attributed to a gang. He made sure his followers planted exactly the right evidence to lead investigators astray.

You can't catch someone without evidence, or an established pattern of behavior. He couldn't count the number of times he put someone in jail based off something insignificant, like the killer kept going to the same laundromat at the same time every week, or a serial arsonist who bought several Bic lighters from the gas station two blocks from his own house but never bought cigarettes.

Criminals, they say, are stupid. Theo learned that the people who say that are also stupid: only the ones who get caught can really fall under that label. Hackers, white-collar criminals, extortionists, spies, these were all criminals who routinely escaped capture, for days, weeks, or months, if not entirely.

The couple from Black Haven, last name Baumann, had sent over their son's computer, as agreed. Like most young men, his computer had little of interest. Mostly pictures of ex-girl-friends, web searches for pornography (some of it normal, some of it downright disgusting), and pirated music. Nothing significant enough to warrant further investigation.

Chelsea's disappearance did, however, warrant such investigation. None of his other victims had vanished so completely. Now she was out there suffering the death of her parents, probably alone, and he couldn't find her. He couldn't harness that anguish, nor go through the rites that would properly channel that pain into his future power.

"Grand Master?" Harmony said from the doorway, appearing without a sound, as usual. "Are you all right? You look troubled."

She spent more time in his office than any other members of the Order, but the acolytes knew better than to circulate rumors. Were the Grand Master to want to be in a relationship with her, they would have no right to judge, and some would have been envious of her position (no matter what her position was). If they were not romantically or physically involved, then pointless speculation would not help anyone.

He sighed, leaning back in his chair, the edges of his fingertips hovering on the edge of *The Black Tome*.

"I have to admit, I am. I don't...It bothers me, knowing the Vessel has, once again, evaded our pursuit."

One of the most challenging things any man or woman is tasked with is the balancing act they must engage in when dealing with separate roles and identities. Pay too much attention to one and the others falter, leading to a swift plummet. Theodore walked his tightrope knowing that he was simultaneously Grand Master of the Order of Nyoru, and an FBI agent. It was almost convenient he did not have a wife or child living with him anymore, as these two roles alone encompassed the entirety of his life. It was a life he had chosen, and it was a life he enjoyed, but keeping his identities separate had become a difficult task indeed.

"Forgive me for questioning, but hasn't the Vessel been eluding us for quite some time already? It seems as though this stress you're under is new. Not that you have to share any details with me, but I have heard that the burden of power can be taxing."

Harmony was unique in that her voice never faltered, as if she planned exactly what she would be saying days before saying it, giving her time to rehearse the tone and timber in which to speak. Theo wondered how the girl stayed so centered but could not ask; to do so would potentially reveal weakness, show to others that he himself was not centered, but he had to be centered.

"I'm sorry, yes, you're right, the Vessel has eluded us for a while now. It's simply…out of character for me to let someone I'm after get away."

Giving a quiet smile, she said, "I'm sure you'll succeed eventually. But…you're not just talking about the Vessel, are you?" He replied with silence. "I've seen the picture on your desk. Your wife, yes? And your son?"

He nodded. "Gone. Both. My fault, too."

She stepped fully into the room and shut the door. "I won't pry. That's your story to share, if you choose. Family can be forgiving. Of course, if you betray family…Well, I believe *The Inferno's* deepest circle of Hell was reserved for betrayers. Yet, our Saint teaches us to embrace pain, to learn from it, does it not?"

Theo pinched the bridge of his nose. Who was she to teach him about his own religion? "Harmony, why exactly have you come to speak to me?"

Tenting her fingers in front of her, she said, "We have a possible location on the Vessel."

Glaring at her, the Grand Master stood. "Why didn't you

tell me this the instant you entered this room?"

"As I said, you looked very stressed before, and I didn't want to trouble you. You have made it clear that you do not wish to go out to get the Vessel yourself, that it would be too compromising, so rather than risk disturbing you and losing valuable time, I immediately sent two of our men to investigate. We set up a tripwire at the safe houses he's visited in the past in case a sudden departure forced him into a desperate situation, and our sensors indicate that a car triggered one roughly half an hour ago. The cabin in question has not been used by others in many months and is in a state of disrepair. While I cannot guarantee that it is him, I can assure you there is a possibility of it. He's never used the same place twice, though, so I only sent two, so as not to tie up the rest, should he definitively surface." *And because all of this is insane. If I had anywhere else to go, I'd leave. Guess I'll bring the Order crashing down around me.*

Again, with her cool, collected voice—her ability to stay calm, even if it made her sound robotic at times. As it was, his face was flushed, and he had become angry at the mere thought of having delayed recapturing the Vessel. She appeared not to react to anything that was going on, even his obvious signs of turmoil.

"Thank you, Harmony." He adjusted the collar of his shirt. "What else do you know about the situation?"

"Only that our men should arrive there in about an hour. They are to call me when they have captured the Vessel, but if you like, I can inform them to call you instead."

Theo stared into nothingness. "I have quite a bit of work to do. Check with me when you hear from them. If I do not appear too busy, let me know what the outcome was."

Angling her head, Harmony asked, "Do you not think they'll be successful?"

He scowled. "My faith in our members is not the problem. The Vessel is crafty, and he has escaped us many times before. Tonight, we may have the advantage, as we've never been able to track him down so soon after he has fled a location, but based on past experience, I will not get my hopes up."

"Nyoru will rise soon, I truly believe that. I know you do, too. Don't give up, Grand Master." She gave him a faint smile and disappeared from the room, opening and closing the door so quietly that she may very well have phased right through it, disappearing into the silence.

Chapter 13

Chelsea restrained the urge to scream as she bolted upright, hand clamped over her mouth. She rarely had nightmares, the exception being during times of stress, this obviously being one of them. In this particular beauty, she was handcuffed to a table, Jordan, Priscilla, and Teresa surrounding her, their fingers replaced by knives. They exchanged fleeting glances, with ticks in their expressions the only clue to the thoughts they were not voicing. Without a sound, they began carving into her, slicing away strip after strip of skin until she was nothing more than a gasping bag of meat, muscles exposed, nerve endings hanging and exposed to freezing air.

Turning the knives on themselves, they sliced down their own sternums, prying themselves open and revealing mirrors within. In each, she saw herself, but no reflection was the same. In one, she was nothing but a head, a translucent skull exposing a rotting brain, thick and dark abscesses stretching back across gyros, pus oozing from every lobe. In another, her flesh dripped from her bones, exposing the bleached skeleton within, organs bursting as she struggled against her captors, each scrap of flesh giving off a plop as it fell to the floor. In the third, the mirror directly in front of her, she was nothing but eyes and a nervous system, doomed to see and feel but never to act, a creature of pure sight and pain, one that would forever be watching, feeling only what it is told to.

The soft *thud* of a car door drew her attention. *What is he doing out there?* she wondered, glancing toward Dave. A thin beam of moonlight fell across his sleeping form.

There was a faint crunching of footsteps across gravel.

Shutting her eyes, she hissed, "Dave! Dave, get up!" Opening them, she saw he was still asleep, so she hopped out of bed, shut her eyes, and nudged him.

His fist wrapped around her shirt collar, then released her again. "Wh-what do...?"

"You hear that?"

He paused. *Crunch*. "Hide under the bed. Now."

Giving a quick glance around the room, Dave curled up in the fireplace, where there was no moonlight to reveal his position. Chelsea followed his instructions and hid under the bed but noticed a faint illumination that could give her away. Part of her wanted to brainstorm a different plan, but she ignored that. Dave had been doing this far longer, so she figured he knew best.

Ignoring the dust, Chelsea wedged herself under the narrow gap between bed and floor. There was a faint creak as two sets of footfalls entered, a flashlight shining around.

"Where is the Vessel?" a man whispered, footsteps clomping through the otherwise empty cabin.

"I dunno," the second said. "Can't see any..."

The men hushed. Their footsteps drew closer and Chelsea thought, *Damn it!*

"You best come out from under there." The first guy tapped his foot near her head. "We've got you. Game over, buddy."

Whimpering, Chelsea tried to ignore the pounding of her heart—and then realized, maybe this time, emotions could be advantageous. At least, if she picked the right ones. Wriggling out, she deliberately stirred up dust, getting it in her eyes and causing them to water. Once the tears were flowing, she sniffed and made half-choking sounds, standing but drawing back to sit on the bed.

"W-w-what do y-you guys want?" Years of watching other

women fake tears gave her a playbook on how to behave now. She didn't feel afraid. Not really. After the last few days, two random goons barely scratched her emotional depths. "I-is this y-your place?"

"What the hell?" the second whispered. "It's not him! Damn it, we drove an hour for nothing!"

"The drive isn't what we should be worried about. Maybe we should bring her back, though. Give the Grand Master someone to work over in the meanwhile."

The second raised an eyebrow. Looking at Chelsea, he shrugged. "You seen a tall, shady guy around here?"

Now a pang of worry ran through her. The Ghost worked alone, didn't he? Or she? Or whatever? Who were these people? Like hell would she go quietly to get 'worked over' by some freakish cult. 'Grand Master' and all that.

"N-n-no." Her voice shook as she glanced around the cabin, looking for a means of escaping or fighting back, even as Dave loomed up behind them.

"Why are you here, then?" Man number two didn't seem to be buying her act.

She didn't bother responding. Dave put one in a headlock and eye-locked the other. A flash lit the cabin as he shot the cat memory into the other man, reducing him to tears as the first slumped in his grasp. Grabbing his bag of supplies, he yelled, "Grab what you can and run!"

Chelsea snatched her bag and the lantern, sprinting out the door after him. A clomping footfall let her know one of the two was chasing or trying to. The goons had parked their car about fifty feet away from Dave's, but didn't block it in, no doubt intending to steal his car, too. Leave no evidence that someone went missing here. The back had a bundle of rope and a bottle that she suspected was chloroform, but Chelsea couldn't read the label. She sure hoped it was, though.

Lighting the lantern's flame, Chelsea hurled it into the attackers' car, shattering it against the center console. Gas spilled out and ignited the seats. She threw herself into the back of Dave's car, holding tight to her bag as he peeled out, spraying rocks and dirt as they bolted down the dirt road. Behind them, the men were stumbling from the cabin, one half conscious, the other helping him along.

From behind them came an explosion so loud that she felt her heart almost break through her chest. Dave maintained steady control of the car, the shock on his face the only indicator he'd noticed. Continuing to bounce over rocks and depressions in the road, he glanced back, saw the inferno behind them, and slowed to a pace that someone might vaguely define as 'safe.'

Deafened by the explosion, he yelled, "WHAT WAS THAT?"

Somewhat giddy, Chelsea grinned, trying to talk over the ringing in her ears. "I BLEW UP THEIR CAR." She'd saved their lives. She'd saved them with science and cunning, not Dave's *Let's hide and maybe use you as bait so I can knock them out from behind* tactic.

"WHAT?"

"I BLEW UP—"

"I HEARD YOU, I'M JUST SURPRISED. WHAT THE HELL DID YOU DO?"

Buckling herself in, Chelsea noticed her hands trembling from both fear and excitement. "I THREW THE LANTERN INTO THEIR CAR. FIRE, CAR, BOOM!"

"DAMN IT!"

"WHAT?"

"I LIKED THAT LANTERN."

He looked back, flashing a broad grin. Laughing aloud, she rolled down the back windows and let the wind rush through her hair, like she would on long family car rides to Six Flags. They drove wordlessly and without the radio until their hearing returned.

"Okay, I think my ears work again." Dave returned to a

normal volume, wiggling a finger in his ear. "Seriously, how did you do that?"

Leaning forward, she wrapped an arm around the headrest, hugging the seat. "I noticed a brown bottle in the back of their car, figured it was chloroform. That stuff explodes on high impacts and under extreme heat. Figured I'd take a chance on disabling them for a while."

Letting out a long, slow breath, Dave shook his head, stunned. "Pretty high payoff for a chance like that. Maybe we should go gambling." They turned onto a highway.

"Good, I already know how to count cards. Never got to do it for real though!" Smiling, she wondered if near-abduction experiences were supposed to be so fun. Shrugging it off, she chalked it up to adrenaline and pyrotechnics.

"If you never got to, why do you know how?"

"Dad used to run poker games. I wanted in, but he said I didn't know how to play, so I taught myself all I could learn. He let me play one game. Just one. I annihilated them. It was *awesome*." The full moon drew her attention, hovering over them like a white sickle.

A sniff brought her head around again as she noticed the glint of a tear on Dave's cheek. "Hey, hey!" She wiped it off. "What's going on, man?"

Shaking his head, Dave didn't seem to want to answer, but she insisted. "He was your dad, but I took the pain of losing him. Now, it doesn't hurt you to talk about that stuff."

"So?"

Enunciating, he repeated himself, "It doesn't hurt *you*."

The strangeness of it all took an extra second for her to process, but when it did, she almost smacked herself for not figuring it out sooner. "Of course. You feel all the pain you take, just like I felt the cat thing."

"Yup." He checked the rearview and turned onto an exit ramp. As they emerged onto another highway, he sped up, a little over the speed limit. Nothing but empty road all around.

Going too fast would land him in a speed trap. Didn't feel the need to rush anyway. Not this time. "I tried explaining it to someone once, a long time ago, when I was a kid. An old friend. Don't remember his name now, but he had no idea what I was saying. I guess you're smarter than him, huh?"

"Smarter than a little kid? I sure hope so." She snorted. Clearing her throat, she added, "But also, you did it to me. Both gave and took away. The explanation had context. It went with the experience. If you had explained it first, I would've thought you were crazy. I did, kinda, at the bar."

Dave glanced over with a smirk. "Thank you for your honesty. Most people are afraid to say what they really think."

Turning her eyes to the empty road ahead, she said, "Is that how you feel, or something you picked up along the way?"

"Both," he said, a little too quickly. "Even as just me, I know people aren't upfront. I mean, you see it all the time. It's so common that people make jokes about it. The age old, 'Do I look fat in these jeans?' line, where it's said no man can honestly answer. If he says yes, she gets mad, because he's saying the jeans look bad on her. If he says no, she assumes she looks fat in other pairs of jeans. If he doesn't answer, it means he thinks she's fat in general. The man can't win, according to the media. I don't believe that's true for everyone, like TV makes it seem, but I'm sure a few people have been in that situation before."

"Do I?" Chelsea said, half joking, half wondering.

"Do you what?"

"Look fat in jeans?"

"You're wearing sweatpants," he said without needing to look around.

He's observant. "But in general."

"I can't say I've looked at you that way. But I don't look at anyone that way."

"No one?"

He shrugged. "Sex appeal, physical beauty…I don't know, I guess they aren't things my eyes were meant to see." Flashing a smile, he added, "But seriously. That stuff's never seemed important, and with me trying to lay low, skipping town all the time…"

"Ah," she said, "so it's like asexuality as a defense mechanism. I get it. I'm not attracted to people much either."

A blank look came over his face. "Sure."

She giggled. "You're not attracted to people because your brain knows you can't form a meaningful relationship."

He made a quiet "Oh!" and then, louder, said, "Yeah, that's about right, I guess. Speaking of that…"

"I know, I'm gone at the next city."

"The hell you are. You stay with me."

Brain momentarily tripping over this new information, she looked over at Dave, whose face was set, dark but determined. He was a gargoyle, scowling down at the world.

"You mean it? Is this 'cause I saved your life?" she teased.

"A little," he gave a half smile, "but also because they know your name, face, where you last lived, and that you were with me. They'll report that to their superiors and come after you, too, and they have resources beyond those of any other civilian organization."

"How do you know that?"

The car was quiet. No one spoke; there was only the sound of wind rushing by and tires thrumming over asphalt.

"They've hunted me a long time. I've put you in danger. Maybe they wouldn't have found you if you fled on your own."

"Or I could be dead already. But together, we can probably do alright."

"Right, we can beat them, sort of. By running away."

"There's gotta be an alternative. We'll find it someday."

Blowing out a slow breath, he trained his eyes on the road. "I sure hope so."

The pair chatted for a while longer, but as conversation tapered off, Chelsea lay down in the backseat, head on her travel bag as Dave turned the radio on, playing the news softly. This

time, sleep eluded her, and she stared out the window at the
pale crescent above, the Reaper's scythe gleaming down from a
wide expanse of darkness.

Chapter 14

Harmony paced her room, running a hand along her head over the tightly pulled strands of white hair. Like most of those who were deemed 'crucial' to the Order of Nyoru, she had her own quarters, tucked neatly away in one of the winding hallways. Hers was on a lower level, not quite near the Grand Master, but close enough. They worked as an inverted hierarchy, with the top members being on the lowest level. She wasn't at the bottom, but she was pretty far down. Only trusted members got to live in the HQ—others were put up at remote houses that could be broken down and wiped clean in half an hour or less, in case suspicious eyes got to prying.

Tonight was an especially troubling one, given how distracted the Grand Master had been. She knew he was lying but didn't know what about. The Order had been a place of safety for her, a group of people who accepted her when others wouldn't, so she hid the fact that she didn't share their beliefs—especially now that she *wanted* to leave, to escape all the delusional crap the other Order members kept spouting on about. The last person to try to leave had his legs broken and was locked away in an adjoining building, cryptically referred to as the Hall of Penance. Others called it the Armory. No one would explain why—the Grand Master once said she "didn't have the right clearance level," but that was all he'd say about it, and seemed to regret the way he worded it.

Her stomach churned at the thought that his distraction might be over learning about her lack of faith, not that she'd told anyone or written it down. Still, she knew there was a lot to the world that couldn't be explained. It wasn't unreasonable to think he'd found a supernatural way of gleaning that information. Her position was that *his* beliefs were unreasonable. She, too, had read of 'Saints' in various shadowy corners of the web. Who knows what they could do?

As it was, he'd be too distracted by this turn of events. Staring at the phone in her hand, she counted *One, two, three…* and when she got to ten, raised it to her ear.

"Say that again, Elijah?"

"The Vessel wasn't alone. He was there, at the cabin, with the girl. Chelsea Valenti, from White Plains, where you said he might be hiding. The one the Grand Master's looking for. Guess we spooked them both, huh?"

Something certainly did, but what? Still, she could play this to her advantage. If the Grand Master didn't know the two were traveling together, she could manipulate the situation more easily.

"Please describe her."

"Uh…she was…it was dark in there, cold, too. I saw light hair, I think. White, but maybe that was the moon. I couldn't make much else out. I'm sorry."

She groaned, continuing to pace. "And what took you so long to report in?"

"Yeah, I'd…I'd rather…not say, because…"

"I need your full and prompt disclosure if there's any hope for your continued service." She caught a glimpse of her red eyes in the mirror.

"We left our phones in the car, like ya said, didn't want them goin' off when tryna catch him, but when we saw the girl, we thought it was a false alarm. He jumped us and ran off, but…One of them blew up our car. Phones got destroyed."

Straightening up, she focused her breathing and slowed the overzealous thumping in her chest. This was no time to be angry at the failure of her underlings. "So where are you now?"

"Rest stop, off Route 280. Uh…Not sure what it's called. We'll figure that out."

"Wait, that's by Livingston. How did you get there? That's miles from where the tripwire went off."

"We hitched a ride; truck driver picked us up."

Well, at least they had the sense not to flag down a state trooper.

"You figure out the place's name and call me back. I'll send someone to get you."

"We could call a cab. It's no trouble."

"You absolutely are not taking a cab to our damn headquarters! What part of 'secret location' and 'privileged eyes only' don't you understand? Figure out your exact location. Report in. That's all. Nothing else. Understand?"

Ending the call, she laid back on her bed and stared at the ceiling, hands covering her eyes. They had been *so close,* and she really wanted to see the look on the Grand Master's face when he found out his 'vessel' had no powers, but that couldn't happen without having the guy there, in front of everyone. Then, after the GM had been discredited, she could leave without fear of repercussions. No one worships a man after learning he has no power.

"Damn it," she whispered. Being shunned by mainstream society would have been preferable to being locked away in the Order's headquarters—not that the members couldn't leave, but an albino would have to have a seriously good reason, between the sunburn and the attention she'd draw. As such, she only went above ground a few times a year to buy clothing and books and similar things. Can't exactly ask Amazon to ship to an unmarked building in the woods. They ran off solar panels and geothermal systems, among other off-grid tech.

Harmony had been there for so long that she nearly couldn't tell whether her paleness was her albinism or a profound lack of sunlight. Not that she'd ever really gone out in the sun, but now she almost missed the light, the heat, even the burns.

A pair of prescription sunglasses lay in the bedside drawer. Reaching in, she pulled them out, flicking open the temples
and sliding them onto her face. Harmony's waist-length braid
of bone-white hair disappeared beneath her favorite red sweat-
er as she threw it on. She'd learned long ago that dark glasses
and a colorful jacket made her look eccentric without drawing
attention to the contrast of her skin tone.

This was a reflection she could live with. In the mirror,
she smiled at herself, enjoying the way she could still blend in
with the world above. She looked more like a fashion icon than
anything else, just not one so glamorous that others would turn
to watch her go.

Shaking her head, she pulled off the glasses and jacket. It
might be a long time before she truly left the HQ. Until then,
every trip above would be a torturous little jab of freedom.
She'd leave someday, that she knew. She had to disprove a god
first.

Chapter 15

Day had barely broken, but Dave and Chelsea were wide awake. They'd stopped at an old rest station, a squat, brown one with no cars or security guards. Slipping up to the doors, Dave yanked out the cables and picked the locks on the doors, which had been held shut with simple padlocks rather than the more technical systems found in modern places. The station was one that time had lost, a relic of the past that none could bother to throw away. By most accounts, it wasn't worth the effort to destroy.

For the wandering duo, it was the perfect place to catch their collective breath, to stop for a moment and discuss logistics—after they relieved their bladders. The place was grimy and dark, like something from a cheap slasher flick, but still, rest was rest, and they needed some. Chelsea thanked herself for remembering gloves.

"So, as you already know, my name's not really Dave," Dave said, drawing a pair of scissors. With a few quick snips, he cut apart his driver's license.

"Yeah. Obvious to people who watched closely enough. So, just me." She spoke quietly, no longer on edge from their flight from the cabin. What had been a combination of fear and excitement gave way to a fatigued emptiness. She hadn't slept well since the 'mother of all surprise parties,' as she was calling it, and the fact was rapidly catching up on her. "If you're not Dave, what's your real name?"

"I'll be going by," he rifled through a variety of fake licenses, "Steve Thompson."

"But your *real* name? Everybody's got one."

"It's best if we don't refer to each other by any other name. I obviously didn't think of myself as Dave enough if I missed responding to it half the time, so I'm Steve now. Just Steve. Call me that. Don't think of yourself as Chelsea either. You're…well, you're no one right now, not until we get you a fake ID. Keep calling yourself something else, some average, ordinary name. It'll reduce confusion, keep you in character. I'll call you Nameless for now. Until one of us decides on a name or gets you a fake."

"But your name?" Nameless insisted, digging her nails into her palm.

"Steve, last name not important. Let's focus on getting us out of here." Gathering up all evidence of his most recent life, he tucked them into a Chinese food take-out carton and lit it on fire, letting it burn in one of the bathroom sinks once he'd disabled the fire alarms.

"It just…bothers me."

"Not knowing something, you mean?"

She picked at a hangnail. "Something else you picked up on?"

"Yup. Didn't need powers for that one."

Cheeks flushing, Nameless sat down on an old bench next to a vending machine. Steve glanced at the door and back to the machine beside her, then shook his head and went outside, indicating he'd be right back.

Getting up, Nameless looked at the contraption, analyzing its plexiglass front and metallic sides. Glancing around, she unplugged it, and then grabbed a piece of hard plastic off the ground. The piece was thin enough to wedge in the gap between the button panel and the rest of the machine. She wriggled it around and popped the panel off. Reaching inside, she found the lever portion of the lock and managed to release it, swinging the front open.

The station door creaked open. "I don't have much money, but we need food. We can stop at…" Steve stopped, staring at Nameless and the unlocked vending machine.

"You were saying?" She smiled, feeling a little less helpless.

"I was saying that you, Nameless, are a very talented young woman."

"Thanks. Maybe you could call me Elizabeth or something. If you're going to get me a fake anyway, you can get a fake with my chosen name on it, right?"

"Elizabeth it is." He reached inside and began pulling out snacks one by one.

Elizabeth tapped him on the shoulder and held up a finger, motioning for him to pause. Plugging the machine back in, she hit the stock purge button inside the machine. Each slot emptied its contents. Holding a travel bag open, he laughed as the cache fell in, filling it up.

"That would've taken me forever." His tone was all the compliment she needed.

"Probably closer to twelve minutes, but okay."

"Whatever." He started scooping up the items that missed the bag. "Could you see if the box has burned up by now?"

Nodding, she disappeared into the men's room, momentarily dizzy at the stench of God-only-knows-how-old piss and grime. The floor was vaguely sticky with what she hoped was humidity and dirt. In the only working sink smoldered the remnants of what she'd once assumed was an average guy. The ash was a stark reminder that Dave had never existed, and she knew little more about the man she was traveling with than she did a stranger. All she knew was that he might not be human. Not entirely. This profound lack of information made Elizabeth grit her teeth, jaws aching from the frustration.

Sifting through the debris, she found a few shards of his driver's license still intact, so she gathered them up and washed the ash down the drain. Returning to Steve, she held out the remains, which he tucked into his pocket, saying he'd destroy them later. Once back in the warmth of the car, they buckled themselves into the front seat.

"So, Elizabeth," Steve said, "how does it feel to be a new woman?"

"I'll feel a bit newer once I get a chance to shower." Exhaustion began creeping into her voice as her eyelids fluttered.

"Yeah." He sounded tired, too. "I could use one myself. You can go first when we get there, though." They turned onto the highway.

"Get where, exactly?"

"Oh! Sorry, when I stepped out before, I was calling about apartments. There's one available in this coastal city in New Jersey. Affordable enough, easy to blend in there. We were heading north before, so going southeast will throw them off."

"I've always wanted to live by a beach. Not under these circumstances."

"Eh." He shrugged, turning on the radio and finding a jazz station. She didn't know the radio still had jazz. "I figure we gotta take what we can get. The possibility of imminent death shouldn't stop you from enjoying what life you have left."

"You really think so, huh?" Elizabeth looked over.

Steve nodded. "People drop dead of heart attacks and aneurysms and bee stings at random, pretty much every day. Us... At least we know it's coming." His voice sounded both strong and sad at the same time. She imagined that's what a hundred-year-old sequoia would sound like on the day it's to be cut down and turned into paper.

"When you put it that way, it doesn't suck." She raised her brow, looking over. "Much."

He laughed as they settled in for what he knew would be a long ride.

Chapter 16

Harmony lay asleep in her bed, all but invisible beneath her white sheets, when the Grand Master threw her door open. Jerking up, she clutched the sheet to her chest as he curled a finger. "Front entrance, fifteen minutes. Wear dark clothing."

Oh god, what happened? He shut the door as he left, so she scrambled up, stumbling to her dresser as the sheet wrapped around her leg. Though she rarely wore anything that wasn't white or red, she did have yoga pants and a long-sleeved black shirt, which she hastily threw on. It was an Order mandate to keep a set of work boots on hand, in case of emergency, as all members would be expected to assist. These were black as well and she shoved her feet into them.

Taking a moment to breathe, she ran cold water and splashed it over her face before brushing her teeth. The process took about five minutes, giving her another five to center herself before having to leave to meet her furious benefactor. Clasping her hands in Namaste mudra, she envisioned herself in a sea of golden wheat, the stalks bending toward and away from her as she breathed in and out. In her mind, she basked in the sunlight, skin bare beneath a cloudless cerulean sky as a gentle breeze curled around her. She relaxed into the wind and heat, as real in her mind as they could ever be.

When she opened her eyes again, she was no longer anxious and flustered. Smile once again in place, she took her glasses from the drawer and drifted out into the hallway. Even in boots, she glided like a phantom, rarely making more than a soft sigh as she drifted from room to room, upstairs, and finally to the front entrance, where the Grand Master waited with Elijah and Woodrow. Their eyes were sunken and dark, their skin sallow.

"Harmony, come with us." The three members were led outside, around the back of the building, to one she'd only heard whispers of: the Hall of Penance, a flat, stone, one-story structure that likely had basement levels, as the HQ did. Turning back, their esteemed leader said, "You know what this building is?"

She nodded.

"You know what lies within?"

She shook her head.

"Today, you learn. Congrats on the promotion." Theo couldn't have sounded less congratulatory if she'd shot him first.

Unlocking the door, he led them inside. Blank walls, curtained windows, and a bare floor greeted her. The top floor only had this one room. In the center sat a stone stairwell. Gesturing, they walked forward, down into a cavernous tunnel lit only by a series of bare bulbs as he followed behind. The walls were stone, gray and yellow and oddly damp-looking. Harmony felt her skin crawling but focused on the image of herself in the field. If she had light in her heart, she could deal with the Order's darkness.

As the stairs ended, the hall flattened out into a more expansive one lined with what looked like prison cells. "This place was gifted to us by previous followers of Nyoru," the Grand Master said, leading them to an elevator. His tone forbade comments and questions. Harmony tried to ignore the ragged clothing within each cell out of fear she might imagine those who died wearing them. Hitting the button for a lower floor, they descended silently into the earth like bodies in their coffins: unable to object or escape.

The doors opened to a small path, and that path led to a

circular room with seven others branching off the center. It was a spoke-and-wheel design, like many old prisons, and she had a feeling this was carved as such for the same reason. Harmony imagined they'd come from the south, so she had a sense of bearing when the Grand Master led them east.

A metal door greeted them. He unlocked this and led the trio inside to another gray-yellow room, this one rectangular. Two metal table-like structures stood in the center, their backs to each other. They looked like motorized operating tables.

"Elijah." The Grand Master pointed to the left. "Woodrow." He pointed to the right. The men took their positions without objection, eyes trained on the floor.

To Harmony, he nodded, flicking his wrists dismissively toward the men. "Bind them." Leather straps rested on the ground near their hands and feet. Swallowing, she obeyed, hands trembling as she drew them tight and locked them in place. The men said nothing aloud, but when she looked into their eyes, she could see how wide their pupils had become and the way sweat glistened on their brows. While they may have known more about what was to happen, having been there longer and privy to more rumors, she didn't need to have heard the stories to guess it wasn't going to be pleasant.

Stepping back, she said, "Okay, they're strapped in place." She wanted to ask what he was going to do but knew she didn't have a place to do so. The last thing she wanted was to invoke his wrath. So far, he didn't seem to want to hurt her. She wanted to keep things that way.

Heavy footfalls echoed around the chamber as he approached her from behind, placing his hand on her shoulder. "You will bear witness to what is about to happen. These two have relayed the events of last night to me, and you handled your situation appropriately. You did all you could, given the situation. However," he strode forward, "these two know how crafty the Vessel is and should have been prepared for variables. Not only did they allow him to slip away again, but their inattentive actions resulted in the destruction of valuable property. As such, they are being reassigned from active follower to one of the Penitent."

Her eyes fell on the Grand Master's hands, one of which was clutched around a whip. "If they are no longer interested in pursuing the Vessel, then what could their place here be? What kind of purpose could they have?"

Unfurling the whip, he jerked his hand and cracked the end across Elijah's chest. Screaming, the man writhed against his bonds as a spattering of red flicked across the floor, drops of it falling along her face and chest. She resisted the temptation to move and cry out, swallowing hard as her throat threatened to close from the shock. Stepping to the side, she remained as silent as possible, allowing the Grand Master to do as he saw fit.

"Their place in the Order shall be here, as part of the armory." Another crack, and this one more vertical; a spray of blood arced up into the air, some of it painting the ceiling and some of it splashing backward onto Woodrow, who whimpered, but said nothing. Elijah began to cry.

"The armory, Grand Master? I...I'm afraid I don't understand." She fought with her body to maintain control of her voice. It wanted to shake, to expose her own abject horror at the situation, to betray the fact that she was afraid, but now was not the time to risk showing weakness to the head of the Order.

"This place," he brought the whip down along Elijah's legs, "is a place designed to create ammunition for Nyoru. By inflicting pain on traitorous or burdensome members of our organization, or upon those who walk the streets and are burdens to the world around them, we generate pain for our god to use upon his return to this plane. These men will bear as much strife as they can, and when the Vessel returns to us, when we sacrifice his life to release our god upon this earth, they will serve as one of the storehouses of agony for Him to harvest and inflict on others. On those who deserve to suffer more."

Harmony felt like she might pass out. All cults were a little bit off kilter, and she'd known that when she agreed to join the Order, but the Grand Master had never seemed so sadistic. This had never seemed like a Jim Jones situation, never a slash and burn policy. Had there been any indication of what his plans were or what he and his so-called god had been capable of, she never would've joined.

This man…This man is a lunatic! How can people follow him? This thought came closely echoed by another: *How can I stay? How am I ever going to get away?*

The Grand Master rounded on Woodrow, cracking once, twice, a third time across his chest in rapid succession, leaving Elijah to shake with the force of his sobbing while listening to how his partner suffered. They all knew Woodrow would suffer a while longer, then Elijah again, then Woodrow…Until whenever the Grand Master decided he was finished.

"Why…Why do you tell me this?" Harmony said, briefly unable to hide the shock. There was a pause in the whipping, a moment where the men were left to feel the extent of their wounds and wonder how they would fester—a psychological assault that was only going to worsen future injuries.

Stepping forward, the Grand Master laid his hand on Harmony's shoulder, and she was painfully aware of how it was hot with fresh, wet blood. The heat of it seeped through her shirt and into her shoulder, burning her. "I tell you this because I trust you. No other member of the Order has set foot in this building and not been placed in shackles to be made into a future weapon. You, my child, are one of the most capable members of our institution, and I feel you're most suited for aiding our quest."

Harmony forced herself to speak. "Thank you, sir. That means more than you can know."

"As it says in *The Black Tome*, all children of Nyoru are family, but in every family, there are those you can trust and those you cannot. You see it every day on the news: fathers imprisoned for beating their kids, brothers who shoot their sisters, happily married people who cheat and lie, children who…" His lip curled up in a snarl. "Children who take your kindness and mercy for granted, and don't recognize the blessings you bestowed upon them." Walking back to Elijah, he brought the whip down on the man's upper arms, eliciting another series of visceral sprays, some of which inevitably struck Harmony. "This is why we must bring the Saint of Glorious Pain into our realm. It is only through pain and suffering that these people will understand the error of their ways. It is only through violence and vengeance that the dredges of mankind will learn to stop attacking one another. We are among the few good people alive, and it is our duty to make sure our species survives under the guidance of the true god, one who can walk among our people and make them pay for their wrongdoings."

The Grand Master circled back to Woodrow and brought the whip across his face, leaving a gash from his jaw line to his left ear. Harmony looked away for an instant, and then back to the Grand Master. *"The Black Tome says all this?"*

"Of course." Another slash across the man's thigh tore open his pants and sent a thin stream of red into the air. Blood ran down the tables, pooling on the floor below. His boots squelched in it, sticking slightly to the floor; the puddle was reaching her, but she dared not move her feet. "And even if it did not, it's easy enough to turn on the news and see how apathy is tearing this world apart. The Saint will bestow the blessing of complete empathy by bringing suffering to all people. They will feel the pain of those around them. Those who act without regard for others will themselves be tortured most."

Harmony shut her mouth as tight as she could as the Grand Master snapped the whip down on Woodrow another two times. It seemed as though he was about to say something else when his phone began to ring. His phone, so they said, had a signal booster, allowing him to get reception almost anywhere, underground included. No other phone got reception in their headquarters.

Turning, he handed her the whip. "Continue the punishment—I expect to see many more wounds when I return. You are to continue as long as they remain conscious; they are no use to us if they cannot remember the pain we inflict."

Holding the blood-drenched weapon, she stared at the Grand Master as he disappeared. Though he shut the metal door behind him, there was a chance she could run, escape to the surface world, and flee to civilization. She knew better than most that they had the resources to track her, if they wished, but she could do so under the hope they would be too distracted by the Vessel and his new companion to bother with the likes of one runaway member.

Then again, if she left, then every single person in the order—as far as she could know—would be on the Grand Master's side. They would support him until the end of their mission, follow every precept, ritual, and law outlined by their precious tome, and his operation would continue running almost flawlessly.

If she stayed, she would have to inflict unimaginable pain on Elijah and Woodrow, but it would mean that there was someone within the Order willing to stand against it. Someone who could twist their operations and, perhaps, bring them to an end. If these were just the adults playing make-believe that she'd originally thought them to be, there would have been nothing to convince her to stay, but she knew that if she were to turn on the news one day and read about a mass suicide or ritualistic slaughter perpetrated by any member of the Order, she would never sleep again. Every moment of her life from that point onward would be haunted by the ghosts of the people she'd allowed to die by doing nothing.

No one wants to be responsible for another person's death. At least, by staying, she could one day stop all this.

Raising the whip, she stepped in front of Woodrow. "Please forgive me," she whispered, slapping the end down across Woodrow's wrists. She didn't draw blood as she'd anticipated, so she thought more about how the Grand Master had moved and imitated the flick of his wrist. This time, the man's forearm opened in a visceral explosion, skin tearing apart as veins exposed themselves, blood flowing freely from the open wound. He stayed silent.

"You need to scream," she pleaded, but he did nothing. She had no way of knowing if the deranged leader was listening, so she yelled, "Scream!" and aimed for the chest.

Harmony missed and struck his face, opening a wound down the center, gouging into his eye, and splitting his lips open. His scream echoed throughout the room and hopefully well into the chambers beyond. She had to stop herself from screaming, too.

She thought about the Grand Master's words, that she had to continue as long as they were still conscious. He was wrong about humanity needing to suffer to learn to function, this much she knew, and so, too, did these men not need to suffer. But there was no life for them now. She knew from the way they looked to her that this was to be their fate until such time as their god showed up to save them.

She knew, even if their god showed up, these two were beyond saving.

Holding back a sob, she tried not to think about what would have happened if the Grand Master finished the punishment. "I'm doing this for you." She hoped they understood, then swung the whip again.

***

In the north room of the wheel-like dungeon, Agent Jotun was talking rapidly into his phone, grateful for having installed a signal booster in the device. Agent Garcia had called, saying there was a development in the Hounds case.

"Could you repeat that?" Jotun said, eyes wide.

"God, can't you hear? I said there's been a report of a killing up in Manhattan, friends of the vic say he was in deep for a drug debt and suddenly paid it off. No one knows where he got the money. Then one day he starts freakin' out, saying he needs to pay off a loan, wouldn't tell anyone why it was so urgent. His buddy Manuel shows up one night, worried about him, and hears, 'No one rips off the Hounds,' followed by gunshots."

"That's huge!" He was lying. This had nothing to do with the Order, so this had nothing to do with the case. A coincidence at best, a copycat at worst. Someone who'd make a passable, if suboptimal, sacrifice.

"Damn right it's huge, why else would I call you so early on our day off?"

He checked a clock, saw it was nine-thirty, and shrugged. Some aren't morning people. "Good point. You there?"

"Enroute. You?"

"Be there in thirty."

Agent Jotun rolled his shoulders back and closed his eyes. The last thing he needed was an overly complicated day and having been so close to the Vessel mere hours ago had him on edge. Stepping out of the soundproofed room, the Grand Master strode down the hall to where he'd left Harmony a few minutes earlier.

Pushing open the door, he surveyed a room that had been repainted red. The girl was sitting in the blood surrounding Elijah and Woodrow, legs splayed out beneath her. Circling her, he saw that both men were heavily lacerated. They had far more wounds than he'd delivered, speaking to a violence of which he didn't know she was capable. Both men had bled out.

"Harmony?" She didn't respond. "This is fine. There will always be more of our own ready to become weapons for Nyoru."

She didn't respond. Approaching her, he spoke again. "Harmony?"

No, she thought. *What 'harmony' is there in this? Where is the beauty, the life, the love I thought this world full of?*

Her golden fields of wheat were burning, the skies black and thunderous. Even in her mind, her hands were stained, her pale body trembling with hideous, nauseating force. Her agonized wail carried across the crackling of flaming crops, splitting the ground so the ash would be lost in the deep, dark earth.

Pushing herself to her feet, she tilted her bloodied face toward him; her once pure-white braid was now drenched from the neck down, two feet of her hair dripping with the blood of the people whose suffering she just ended.

Discord smiled at him. "Grand Master, truly your forgiveness I implore, but these men were loudly squawking, and so gently you came walking, ah, so faintly you came talking, that I scarce was sure I heard you." *Here I opened wide the door...*

Part Three:
Hardened Hearts

Chapter 17

Three months later…

Elizabeth was trapped. She'd known this was coming, but there hadn't been a way around it. After considering every option and each angle, there had been no escaping. Unable to move, she sat with her eyes shut, sweat on her brow despite the cool air blowing across her, and wondered what Steve was doing.

Is he thinking about me? Is he back at the apartment, wondering where I am, or smiling to himself, grateful for time alone? Maybe he's reading the newspaper, probably The Link *or the* Asbury Park Press, *with his feet kicked back on the table like I've been asking him NOT to do. At least he doesn't wear shoes when he does it, but still, I get tired of having to clean the table.*

Throwing her head back against the headrest, she yelled, "Move, damn it!" at the traffic in front of her car. She'd gotten a job as a waitress at Friday's, but today they'd let her off *right* when all the beach-bound traffic decided to funnel down Route 36 and into Long Branch. It was like trying to fit a waterfall in a coffee cup.

Pulling out her phone, she punched in Steve's number and shot him a text. Ordinarily she wouldn't text while driving, but in gridlocked traffic, she wasn't really 'driving.'

Hey, sorry I'm running late. Traffic. Don't worry. I know you want to go to the store, but if you text me a list, I'll stop by myself. If you don't, I'll head straight back to the apartment. Either way, see you soon.

Steve had gotten a job working as a cook at a local bar, mostly short order burgers and fries, easy work for a decent enough wage. Their apartment, as he'd said, was quite cheap. It was also in a seedy part of town. Long Branch had as much good as it had bad. It was a yin-yang, with Broadway dividing the two sides, providing no middle ground.

They were fortunate enough to live on the edge of the bad side, which meant cheap rent and a not-overwhelming amount of security concerns. There was the occasional drug dealer walking by, but not enough activity to attract police officers. Those were the real problems. A low-life thug could be dealt with easily. A cop? Far more hassle than they needed.

Elizabeth coasted along in the far-right lane and came up on a small shopping plaza, so she cut into the lot and maneuvered through to a back exit that dumped them onto a side street. Grinning at the traffic-free road, she sped down the flat expanse of blacktop, tapping a little too hard on the accelerator. Backing off, she cruised, cutting down residential roads to avoid the traffic, and made it back in a few minutes. Steve hadn't responded.

Sliding from the dark blue four-door, she cursed her uniform full-length black pants and trudged up the cracked stairs to apartment 4A, their newest safehouse. Opening the door, she found the lights off, sunlight streaming through the window and along the pale walls. Craning her neck, she found Steve asleep on the couch. He opened his eyes as she crossed to the kitchen.

"Sup, Liz?" He stretched his arms overhead.

"Nah much, how's about you, ya lazy bum?" She grinned and pried open the refrigerator to pull out a water. Her companion let out a groan and stood up, continuing to stretch.

"I'm good. I have the supernatural ability to fall asleep anywhere at any given time. Makes the night shifts suck less." Pouring himself a bowl of cornflakes, he sat down at the rickety table they'd snatched from someone's bulk trash pile a few days after moving in.

"Really, that's your superpower?" Her eyebrows drifted up toward her bangs.

"Sure is. You, you're one of them rubber band girls."

She rolled her eyes, still smiling. The first few weeks, they didn't have a real identity for her. Aside from a name, she had no ID or evidence of her existence, so she stayed inside while he went to work and found hook-ups to falsify documents, make her new identity more credible. A combination of not having much money for food and doing yoga to pass the time made her thinner and more flexible—a fact he mocked good-naturedly.

Yoga didn't do it alone. No matter her name, she'd spent years trying to fill an emptiness inside her with reading, friendship, and, from her teen years on, with food. Now, that void didn't bother her so much. It no longer felt like an absence, just a waiting.

These changes, combined with cutting and dyeing her hair herself and getting colored contacts from Steve, made her almost unrecognizable. At her insistence, he'd allowed her to bleach his hair and spray a semi-permanent tattoo sleeve along his right arm. Perfect for throwing off those who knew him before, but didn't keep him marked, allowing him to phase into the next life with ease. He remained lanky, as he'd been before, and she was quick to point that out.

Leaving him to finish his cereal, Liz went to change out of her uniform and shower. French fry grease was a distinct and permeating scent, and it made her queasy if around it for too long. Steve stared out the window, watching cars rush by. Though only a few blocks away, the ocean wasn't visible due to townhouses along the water's edge.

Over the past few months, Steve had managed to 'give away' most of the pain he was holding onto. The occasional drug dealer, gang member, or other criminal delinquent that he caught wind of would receive some traumatic memory or another. Of course, with every person he targeted, he found another set of people hurt by that person, and would, when possible, take their pain away as well. This was done subtly and often from afar. Those he'd come into contact with had no idea he was behind the sudden pain or lack thereof. Like at the cabin, there had been one or two times where Elizabeth caught him off guard, but she'd both learned to step around him more carefully and to deal with emotional disturbances more stoically. Each time hurt a little less.

"Hey!" Liz looked out from the crack in the bathroom door. "Where are all the towels?"

He apologized, saying he didn't fold the laundry earlier and left the folded clothes and towels on his bed. She watched him disappear to his bedroom door, her choppy hair spiked out in different directions. They both had simple bedrooms, amounting to little more than a bed and dresser in each, though his had a laptop (freshly pilfered from a garage sale) and documents on where they might go next and the variety of alternate identities they could assume, and hers had a few stacks of books on subjects ranging from religion and philosophy to physics and psychology. She'd read the majority of them and already marked which ones she wouldn't want to leave behind, carefully dusting for prints to make sure she was leaving evidence in case they had to disappear again in a hurry.

Returning, he handed her a blue towel through the crack in the door, and she disappeared. A few minutes later, she reappeared, hair somewhat drier, with the towel wrapped around her torso. "You did all the laundry, right? Is my stuff still in your room, too?"

Eyes averted, Steve nodded, and heard her footsteps padding around. She came back in a tank top and shorts, fanning herself. "Is the heat supposed to break soon?"

"It's more the problem of the humidity than the heat, but I think so. Thunderstorms coming." Then, more seriously, he added, "Are you okay?"

Arching her brow, she said, "Well, yeah. I mean, it's hot, but I can deal. Besides, we have air conditioning, so that helps take the edge off. Our unit sucks."

Shaking his head, Steve said, "No, I mean…You. Like, emotionally. I want to know how you are doing, coping with leaving White Plains, all that kind of stuff. I want to know without looking you in the eyes and worming around inside your head." He smiled, and she chuckled back at him.

His abilities had become something of a running joke, like when people embrace their love of comic books and become known as the comic book guy. Rather than something one might mock, it was a defining and endearing characteristic. Some had comics, he had eyes that could literally see into your soul. Others had temperamental cats, which would've been far worse for Elizabeth.

Settling back in her chair, Liz shut her eyes. "I have a PhD at twenty-three, and the crowning moment of my recent work history has been when an older woman left that twenty dollars tip because I brought extra sauce with her cheeseburger."

"For what it's worth, you're not the only doctor slinging sandwiches."

"It's worth about as much as my hourly pay."

"Okay, but how about elsewise? Like with your friends, the home you left behind, the cabin incident?"

She shrugged. "It's all in the past, right? Nothing to do but move on."

"Just because you have to move on doesn't mean that you have done so already. Seriously, you okay?"

Nothing would make any of this 'okay,' but she knew, as everyone does, that it would get better with time. The wound would gradually stitch itself closed. Maybe it wouldn't heal, but the ache would fade. "Honestly, I didn't imagine my setting out into the world would be marked by fake names, gridlocked traffic, and minimum-wage service positions. But I'm alive, so I guess I can't really complain about that part.

"And my friends? I may only have had three, but I guess they meant more to me than I realized. I…I feel like I see them everywhere, especially Priscilla. I don't know why her, of all people, but yeah, I miss them. Sometimes I think about logging on to Facebook or shooting them a text when I remember that I can't. Once in a while, I wake up thinking that I'm still talking to them, like we're having a conversation just like old times, and I keep my eyes shut and lay in bed a little longer to hold onto that."

Her gaze drifted out of focus, like maybe, written on the far wall of the universe, she could find an equation that would answer all the questions she couldn't bring herself to ask. "The town…That part doesn't bother me much, but it's funny, the ways you miss the place where you grew up. I never thought it would wander into Stop & Shop and say that I missed Jimmy's Olde Towne Grocery, or that I'd go to some chain restaurant and miss the artery clogging breakfast potatoes from Murray's Diner. This place has history, sure, but it's not *my* history. And…I guess that's okay, since 'I' no longer exist. I am Elizabeth Sorrento, and as far as anyone else is concerned, I have never been anyone else."

Nodding, he waited to see if she would go on, but she didn't. Occasionally, she would open up to him, share her thoughts, but this didn't happen often. She seemed inclined to keep everything inside. Whether this was because it was simply how she decided to work through things or because she didn't want to burden him, he couldn't tell. Since he was the same way, he couldn't exactly blame her.

"Did you…want me to take anything away?" He kept his eyes averted, focusing on the crook of her right elbow.

"No." She shook her head. "Things aren't bad. The occasional twinge of homesickness or heartache, that's all. Nothing to worry about. But I'll let you know, okay? Relax."

They both understood that 'I'll let you know' wasn't about taking pain away from her, it was about giving back the anguish of her parents' death and the little joys that made losing them so difficult. He'd kept that locked up in his heart, keeping hers safe, all this time.

"Alright," he said. "Just making sure. What we go through and how we react changes us and can turn us into something we'd never dreamed of being. Trauma leads to transformation. Sometimes we become better people; sometimes, we become better monsters."

Chapter 18

With the Grand Master away at work, Discord stood to lead mass. As the right hand of the organization, the newly appointed Mistress of Agony, it became her duty to guide the flock when Theo wasn't present. This would be her first time leading the sermon without his guidance, and only the third time *anyone* other than the Grand Master had led. Normally, if their benefactor wasn't present, they were expected to reflect on their pamphlet of selected teachings.

Glowering at the crowd, she felt her internal environment still in disarray. All these months later, the fields still smoldered, the oceans devoid of creatures. The winds blew birds from the sky and lightning struck down all the creatures that attempted to scurry for cover. Attempting to meditate unleashed more of that storm in her heart. She looked down at the chaos, her mind's eye finally fully open to the true grit and turmoil of the world.

Opening *The Black Tome* to a random page, she looked out over the crowd and said, "Welcome, followers of the Saint of Glorious Pain. Our Grand Master couldn't be here. He's busy. Deal with it." An unsteady murmur rippled through the crowd. "Today I read from a lesser-discussed section of *The Black Tome* by which our actions and redemption are dictated."

Disgusting, worthless drivel, she thought. What she said next was not so standard, stemming from her mother's off-beat Buddhist teachings and essays she'd read in passing rather than any Order text.

"Pain is a part of who we are. There is no escaping that. Whether we have it or do not, whether physical or emotional, whether we give it or receive it, we are, to an extent, defined by this four-letter word.

"This does not mean we are doomed to live savage, ago-nized lives. Instead, we can use what we know about ourselves and how we process such sensations to develop stronger bar-riers. We can learn what hurts us and prevent it from doing so. We can work on why we're oversensitive to some issues and move past whatever past trauma so afflicts us.

"In dealing with pain, we can choose to excise it, like a tumor, or pass it on, like a disease. Some of us only want to live in peace. Others only know how to make others as miserable as they are. Many such people are under the impression that 'happiness' is about being less miserable than everyone else; they say that if everyone suffers, but they suffer less, then by comparison, they're doing well. This is not so.

"Society's true order is about accepting who and what we are without feeling the need to change or improve to be satis-fied. It's about understanding our roles and obligations, about balancing wants and desires. About coming to terms with what others have done to us, and what we have done to others."

She paused, reflecting on three months' worth of tortur-ing prisoners, sometimes for information, sometimes for cre-ating 'weapons' for 'Nyoru' to use. Few survived. She couldn't condemn them to imprisonment and anguish. Besides, the few who lived to see a prison cell died from infections and malnu-trition. Mercy delivered through swift death.

"We...are constantly faced with difficulty. We are faced with pain every day, both our own and that felt by others." Continuously glancing down, she hoped she was giving the im-pression of reading. "Pain does not have to be who we are. It is never our sole identity. All things fade, and as we age, as we move from one location to the next, we evolve. We become more complex creatures.

"*The Black Tome* states that when the Vessel shares the fully matured power of Nyoru, it will be only to the Incarnate. When this day comes, the Saint of Glorious Pain will determine who is or isn't meant to suffer. Those condemned will die as Wretches; those saved will live a glorious existence free of all suffering. Those who anger Nyoru will, upon transference of power from Vessel to Incarnate, be damned with an Eternity of Sorrows—not merely one full of pain, but one devoid of hope. All happiness and joy will be ripped away and replaced with the agony they have inflicted upon others." That much was in the tome; she had to read some 'factual' things to convince the crowd this was all in the book.

Returning to her improvisation, Discord said, "Until such a day as Nyoru returns to our world, we must decide whether we will endure, take, or give pain. Whether we are most happy suffering in silence or suffering together. Those who choose wrong must bear the consequences."

Chapter 19

"So, you really think the Hounds aren't just a gang?" Agent Jotun asked, looking around the Manhattan streets. The 'lead' involving the man in debt turned out to be a dead end when they learned the witness was high at the time that he heard the shooting. The alleged dead man turned up at the FBI headquarters to put claims of his death to rest. They'd just left the apartment of another victim. This one had been beaten to death.

Agent Garcia nodded. "Too much shady crap going on. They aren't out running through streets, aren't robbing stores, no drive-bys, no drug rings, but people have been turning up dead for a while now, all of them beaten and starved. It's like they're trying to send some kinda message."

"So, you think it's a cult?"

"Don't give me that face, Jotun. Not unless you have better ideas."

He wrinkled his nose and looked at the ground.

"Why else would people be put back in their homes *after* getting killed? Most people dispose of bodies. Gang, they leave 'em in enemy territory. These people…whoever's doing this wants to say that it can happen to anyone." She'd personally gone to most of the scenes, arriving first on days Agent Jotun wasn't busy, and saw the wounds made on the bodies. The beatings, the floggings, the way some peoples' eyes were gouged out prior to death. It had taken all her restraint and professionalism not to vomit.

She also noticed how Jotun wasn't around in the days prior

to most disappearances. The agent might've been newer to the Bureau than others, but even her rookie eyes saw how he didn't react to pictures of the victims and seemed indifferent to how they might've died, as if he didn't care—or as if he already knew.

Still, she couldn't report 'my partner is weird' to the director. They wouldn't pursue the issue, especially because he was a veteran agent, and her reputation would be called into question. If anything, there'd be a mark in her file saying she had issues with authority. Keeping an eye on the older agent, she added, "These people were all tortured. I don't have much to go on, but I think they were part of some sort of…Some sort of ritual."

"That certainly is a hunch. Not sure if I see it though, doesn't quite look like that to me. I mean, if this were a cult, wouldn't they leave the sign, some sort of mark, an insignia? None of that here. Cults, they want to be known, they want to be heard, even if that means the police kicking down their doors sometimes. These people don't want to be found. Doesn't sound like much of a cult to you, does it?"

"Maybe there are more factors involved. Maybe they see what happens once feds get involved and would prefer to finish their mission rather than have some big dramatic takeover. I mean, whoever's running this must be smart, and gangs usually aren't. These attacks are clearly related, connected somehow, probably orchestrated by a man with a real Messiah complex."

"You think? Put that in the report if you want, but it'll be all you. Others will know that." He narrowed his eyes at her.

Agent Garcia nodded at her partner. "Look at all the people taken. The drug addled, entry-level gang members, petty criminals who got off on probation or plea bargains. We're looking at a well-connected person who can't stand the sight of what the world has come to, the sight of all these people running around causing havoc and getting away with it. This guy probably thinks he's saving them or calling them to a higher purpose."

They were called. They failed to serve.

"Interesting idea. Might make a good novel someday."

She rolled her eyes. "Either way, we have a report to write."

"I have some things to take care of. Why don't you write it up, seeing as you're so keen on your cult theory?"

Agent Garcia sighed. "Sure. No problem, Jotun." She was used to his bailing, especially when it came to paperwork. Hopping into his car, he drove casually away, giving the illusion of having nothing to do. She watched him go, unable to shake the chill that swept through her.

Chapter 20

Liz was doing reconnaissance. At least, that's what Steve called it. The term applied to sun tanning, running, or any outdoor activity where she could blend into the crowd and be unnoticed among the tourists. Regardless, she hid behind a large hat and sunglasses whenever she could. The tan she'd developed from all that 'reconnaissance' work helped hide her identity as well.

She did her best to listen for new information while out among the masses. Steve said it was imperative that they know when major events were going on, like free bobblehead day at Monmouth Park or a charity event at Pier Village, or especially the marathon, which had blocked up roads for hours, nearly crippling all traffic flow in and out of the city.

It was a sunny day without much wind, so she was able to lay on the beach for a while and bask in the warmth before meandering through the crowds. She had to be careful not to fall asleep while lying down, but once up on her feet, the dreamy sensation faded. While weaving through the rampaging children, the women with harsh New York accents, and shirtless old men with flyaway gray chest hair, she heard fragments about the upcoming Blues Festival, and mapped out what roads would be most crowded and when.

Heading south from the Village, she walked along the blacktop toward what locals called West End, which didn't make sense because it wasn't any more west than the rest of Long Branch. Steve was working a dayshift, so she aimed to hang out and wait for his shift to end before hitching a ride home. That involved a mile-long trek in flip-flops, but she shrugged it off. This was a path she'd walked several times in recent weeks. Locals said something about that part of the boardwalk being the 'Moss Mile,' but the city hadn't rebuilt the boardwalk yet. They'd expanded the beach significantly, she heard, but that was all.

While dodging the runners and recent mothers pushing sleeping infants in strollers, she was once again struck by the phantom of Priscilla, who this time seemed to be sitting on a plastic orange divider, staring at the ocean and holding herself. Then she noticed the other walkers gave her a wide berth, indicating she was real and not a daydream, so Liz knew better than to think it was really her.

That is, until she got closer and saw it was, unmistakably, her old friend Priscilla—and that people were skirting around her due to the track marks along the inside of her arms.

"'Scuze me, could you spare any cash? Lookin' for a cab home," Priscilla said to Liz.

"Sorry, no," Liz said, voice shaking. *What do I do? She…Oh God, I can't leave her! But I can't take her with me. What would Steve say?*

She thought back to the bar, to a man who no longer existed talking to a woman who no longer existed: *I can't stand to see innocent people get hurt.*

Quietly, in case she was wrong, Liz whispered, "Priscilla?"

Her eyes slowly widened. "How do you…?" And she glanced around, as if to run.

"Wait, wait," she hissed, already berating herself, knowing that Steve would *also* say *Chelsea Valenti no longer exists*, but Priscilla did, and she wasn't going to walk away. "It…It's me, Chelsea," she said, as quietly as she could.

"Chelsea? It…It really is…?"

A smile spread across her face.

Chapter 21

Theo glared at his computer screen, wondering how *she* managed to disappear. He couldn't select another target. That would be unforgivable, to have primed someone and allow her to escape. No, he would have to track Chelsea down, no matter where she went or what names she assumed. Displayed in front of him was an image of the Long Branch beach, some dopey story about an upcoming music festival accompanying it, but rather than the two people in the foreground of the photo, he was most interested in the background.

Though she had dyed her hair, cut it, and lost a good bit of weight, he'd spent enough time studying people and hunting down those who dared to evade his pursuit to know that this was Chelsea Valenti. He made phone calls and found no one by that name was currently renting rooms in the city, so he had no other choice.

Flipping through the list of friends the Valentis had given him shortly before he killed them, he researched each and found Priscilla was now unemployed and a heroin addict. He had offered her both a job placement and the drug connection, so long as she was willing to relocate—and report any sightings of her old friend directly to him, as soon as she could. He needed a way to keep her anchored. Together, she and the Vessel could be too alert, someone always on guard, watching, readying the next way out. Distracting them would allow Theo to catch them. Well, give him a better chance.

She had readily accepted. Now, all he had to do was wait

and hope that she was more reliable than her addiction suggested.

He didn't have to wait long. His phone chimed with an incoming text message, and opening his phone, he saw, **With Chelsea now. Goes by Liz. Willett you know where lives.**

And a few seconds later, ***Will let.**

Theo smiled, knowing full well that his teeth would be showing, because he wanted so desperately to sink his fangs into the next meal. He couldn't wait to hold her down, to take a knife to that body of hers again and again, to feed on her suffering. Watching her tortured face relax into eternal repose was an unparalleled experience.

"Grand Master." Discord entered without knocking. "We believe we've located the Vessel again. He is still with that girl from before." Today, as usual these days, she was dressed in a white shirt and white shoes with red pants and a thin, red jacket, seeming to make her crimson eyes glow brighter for it. For reasons none of them could figure out, she had never been able to wash the blood out of her hair. That luxurious white braid was stained red at the end.

"Girl from…? What do you mean?" He glanced at the computer screen.

"The girl who distracted our men at the cabin a few months ago. When I tried to tell you about her, you said you didn't care about, and I quote, 'Some idiot girl who happened to get in the way.' I proceeded under the assumption that she may be working with the Vessel in some way or another, following up with some friends of hers, tapping their phones."

The Grand Master's eyes widened. His Mistress of Agony was better at her job than he thought, and it was growing increasingly difficult for him to keep things under his control.

"This girl apparently ran into an old friend of hers, Priscilla, and I've currently got her tracked to some sort of bar and grill down in Long Branch, New Jersey. About an hour's drive from here. We can send them down, have them survey the location, bring the Vessel back as soon as possible."

He couldn't tell her he'd also been pursuing Chelsea. The ordained sacrifices were *his* project, and his alone. Theo chose them, tortured them, slaughtered them, and had never, under any circumstances, tolerated interference.

Then again, maybe it would be more convenient if he were to blend some elements for once. "Bring both the Vessel and the girl back here, alive. Preferably unconscious, at first. I want to know what's so special about her that he felt inclined to bring someone along. This is an extreme deviation for his behavior, and I find myself suspicious. The Vessel was always a loner."

"Always? Are you sure about that?" She cocked her head.

"Of course I'm sure," he snapped. Then, covering his tracks, he added, "I have been following him for many years, long before you entered the Order, and he has never had so much as a single friend. Now, he seems to have a traveling companion, a woman he wants to keep around. I want to know why."

Discord nodded. "As you wish."

The Grand Master looked at his phone, and when he glanced up, the woman in front of him had vanished.

Eyes on the girl on his computer screen, he whispered to her image, imagining she could hear him and know the danger he posed even from afar. "What a fitting coincidence. I get to kill you and become a god in the same breath. Maybe I'll kill the Vessel first, let you witness my transformation...and then as Nyoru, I will bless you with the honor of being my first victim."

Chapter 22

Steve had been glancing over since the moment Priscilla and Liz sat down in his eatery. Liz pointedly avoided making eye contact so he couldn't lock on and find out about her friend. She wanted the opportunity to tell him herself. When it came to matters of life and death, it was bad manners not to deliver news in person.

Still, that didn't stop them from ordering food that Steve would then have to cook. Priscilla ordered a house salad but turned almost as green as the lettuce when it arrived, instead opting to take half-hearted jabs at the leaves with her fork. Liz ordered a steak, medium-rare, and had the sides come in a to-go carton. Throughout the meal, they talked about the last few months (incriminating details left out), Priscilla's track marks, and Liz's new look—namely, "Why cut your beautiful hair?"

Priscilla eyed the alcohol shelf. Liz didn't offer. Neither she nor Steve drank, and her friend certainly didn't need it. In one respect, they avoided booze because they needed to stay attentive in case an attacker came bearing down on them. On the other, they used fake IDs. If someone carded them, there was a chance of them getting caught and arrested. That was a sure way to have the cops figure out they weren't who they said they were.

Smiling at a red-headed waitress, Liz filled out the check, sticking to her rule of *You always have enough money to leave a good tip,* even though she really didn't. She made little, and only had the cash she'd skipped town with months earlier. Priscilla's eyes never left the wad of cash. Liz practically had to drag her to the door.

Once outside, they made their way around the building to the staff portion of the parking lot, waiting on the trunk of the car. Priscilla sat with her legs splayed despite her denim mini-skirt; when Steve arrived, he never once glanced at the woman or what her position may have revealed.

"Liz, hi, who's this?" He never once looked at Priscilla.

The women exchanged a glance. "She's…someone who needs help. An innocent person who's been hurt. A friend." She decided not to use words after all and locked eyes with him, allowing him to scan her thoughts. He felt how much it hurt to see someone she cared about fall on such hardship, then returned that pain to Liz.

Steve nodded. "Okay."

"Maybe she could spend the afternoon at our place, where others can't get to her."

Tapping his foot, Steve forced a smile and feigned playful-ness. "I really don't think that's a great idea. I need to shower, and we haven't vacuumed in weeks. This little thing might get eaten by a dust bunny!"

Giving an equally fake laugh, Liz said, "I'll protect her. What kind of friend would I be if I didn't watch out for her?"

Glaring, he said, "Then…I suppose she should come visit."

***

They walked up the front steps to the apartment building, Priscilla's head twisting and turning all the way to take in the various 'charms' of their 'humble home.' A shirtless man with a profound beer belly turned, staring at her rear and smiling. Two people lingering outside apartment 1C scattered, as peo-ple do when they're interrupted while buying drugs. Priscilla never noticed. Steve rolled his eyes and glanced back at Liz, who shrugged as if to say, *There's a chance she's high.*

Unlocking the door, Steve called back to the guest. "So, Priscilla, tell me about yourself. Liz seems to know you pretty well. What do you do here in town?"

Liz chuckled; she'd come to realize his game by now. He asked lots of questions to make people think he was being friendly. In actuality, he was steering the conversation away from his own life. People love many things, but one of the greatest universal loves people have is the love of talking about themselves.

"Me? I, uh, I work as a nurse, at Monmouth Medical," she stuttered. "I'm an ER nurse. Take care of trauma victims and stuff. They keep me on hand because I'm good with kids."

"Kids, huh?" Steve walked inside. Liz led Priscilla in after him.

Priscilla nodded. "Yeah, I…I guess I really like working with them, you know? Making sure they're safe and not scared. Hospitals…they're scary places sometimes, and kids need to know things are going to be okay."

Steve leaned out from the kitchen, one eyebrow raised. Liz returned it with a very slight nod and then turned to her guest. "Would you excuse me for a sec? I'm going to put coffee on. Would you like any?"

The frail woman shook her head and Liz disappeared into the kitchenette. "Think you can help her?" She took the empty coffee pot and filled it with water.

"Haven't looked at her yet. I don't know. Why?"

Liz bit her lip, dumping the water into the machine and scooping grinds into the filter.

Tapping her shoulder, Steve asked, "Why?" more forcefully than before.

Glancing back at her friend, Liz shook her head. "I… Never mind, it's stupid."

She hit the power button and turned to leave but he grabbed her hand. "You've never done a stupid thing in your life. What are you thinking?"

Setting her jaw, she readied herself for his mocking retort. "If you take whatever it is that makes her...you know...I...I want you to give it to me, so I understand. I know it's odd, but she always had her act together. She was so secure and smart and stable...Never saw this coming. At all. I need to know what went wrong. Please humor me."

Mouth agape, he tried to process what she said. She *wanted* her pain? The pain that drove her to drug use? "Odd...barely covers it. Most people spend their lives running from pain. You still haven't taken yours back yet."

"I know, I know, and I'm sorry," she sighed. "I feel like... like I need to know."

He shook his head. "You'd really put yourself through hell to satisfy your curiosity?"

"Yeah."

"You must've been a cat in a past life." Steve turned to look out at Priscilla. "Only if I think you can handle it."

She nodded. "I can."

The coffee pot beeped; she poured herself a cup and sat down with Priscilla as Steve went to shower. As Liz sat down on a nearby stool, Priscilla finished typing out a text message and put her phone down.

"So...this...is your life now?" Priscilla said. "Run around with Stan—"

"Steve."

"—and do...whatever?"

It was Liz's turn to play the game. "I do what I want, yeah. So do you, it seems." Priscilla drew back, covering her bruises. "Hey, I'm not judging you. Really, I'm not. I want to understand."

Unable or unwilling to look up, Priscilla tightened her grip on her arm. "Really?"

"Yeah, really. I mean, I know a lot of stuff, but I don't know why you're doing this. You used to be a close friend of mine, but I never thought you'd do drugs. Never at all. I want to know why, but I get it if you don't want to tell me."

The girl didn't seem to want to respond, but she didn't change the topic either. She didn't say anything.

Liz grimaced. "Look, I sympathize. Maybe you used to forget things, or maybe for fun. I don't care, Priss. I want to make sure you're safe. Hell, you can look me in the eyes and say, 'I'm a user, but I don't share needles and I make sure not to overdose.' If I believe you, you go on your way. I won't stop you. I'm not a cop, I'm not a parent, I'm a friend, no matter what my name is."

They sat in silence for a few minutes as Liz waited for Priscilla to answer. Her coffee gradually stopped steaming and the shower ceased running. Taking a sip, Liz locked eyes with her friend.

Rubbing her exposed arms, Priscilla's lip trembled, eyes glazing over.

"I…I've been using for years."

Letting her head sink into her hands, Liz took a long whiff of her drink.

"Why didn't you tell us?" She stared into her cup.

"It wasn't a big deal." Priscilla curled her legs beneath her. "A needle between my toes once in a while, just to take the edge off…It helped me keep focused. Ride the edge, keep the grades, keep all the pieces together."

"And now?" Liz took a long swig, eyes unblinking.

"Now, I…I can't focus without it."

Steve crossed to his room to get changed as Priscilla's phone went off.

"Need to get that?" Liz said, having almost forgotten what it was like to get a real text message. Steve's amounted to 'Get milk' or 'Running late' or, infamously, 'Someone crapped on front steps, take back steps to car today.'

Priscilla glanced at it and grimaced as Steve walked up be-hind her, catching a glimpse of the screen. His eyes narrowed and he walked around the couch, kneeling in front, and locking eyes with her. The phone fell from her hand.

Liz tensed, her body a bundle of nerves that, while not hard-wired like his, knew to be ready for something. "What's going on?"

"You really want to know everything?" He turned. She locked on his mirror-like eyes and the tunnel closed in around them. Priscilla's memories crashed down.

At the back of her mind she knew that her dad had loved her, but that didn't stop the feeling of this vast, aching distance from invading her heart and chilling every inch of her body, just like it didn't stop the sting of Mother's slap or the burning shame that threatened to leave her world in ashes as the wench broadcasted every excruciating detail of her life—whether or not those details were true—on social media or in person, just for laughs.

Guess who wet the bed last night, at thirteen years old?

Oh, is that Jamie Lancaster? He's way out of your league.

Maybe if you didn't eat seconds, you wouldn't be such a fat pig.

Liz had never wanted to hurt her mother, or disagreed with her in any way, but if her mother had been alive and present, she would've screamed at her, despite knowing the feelings weren't her own. Beneath that was the ache, the cold, the desperation; it was something that felt pitch black and echoed in her heart like the ringing from listening to a jackhammer break up concrete. A new void, not like her own, something writhing and active and frenzied, filled her. She knew what Priscilla wanted, what it felt like to want heroin that badly, what it felt like to *need* something to feel anything other than that horrible black hole to which she'd become accustomed.

And then, beneath that still, a deal. A flicker of warmth as terms and conditions were worked out. A stranger who offered Priscilla an exchange to never be without her fix again—so long as he could have *his* fix. The man was hooded, had glasses on, kept his face turned away. The world was distorted through the rusty haze of a speedball buzz, colors blooming in and out of existence; there was no way to recognize who the man was. A shadow seemed to have swallowed the periphery of her memory-vision, and any guilt she may have had at revealing 'Chelsea's' location was overshadowed by the almost excruciating joy that came from thinking of her next dozen scores.

"You wanted to know," Steve growled.

Liz was pissed at a great number of people, but she knew her own rage and pain from that of Priscilla. She debated slapping her so-called friend. There was a better, more lasting option.

"Give this crap back to her," Liz snarled, locking eyes with Steve. Then the pain was gone, and he was looking at Priscilla again, whose fleeting, open, honest smile shattered as the light she'd briefly found was blotted out again. Her mouth gaped, eyes darkening, hand shaking, about to lose her tenuous grasp on her salvation.

Glancing at his watch, Steve walked to the window. "You met her, what, two hours ago? A little more? They could be right around the corner."

"Damn you, Priscilla!" Liz raced to her room, shoving what clothes she had into a bag, her necessary books into another. The process took sixty seconds at most.

"Wh-what? What did I do?" she said, rising to her feet on shaky legs. "He said—"

"We know what he said!" Steve and Liz both yelled. Rushing to the door, Steve opened it then jerked back, slamming it shut.

"They're here?" Liz hissed. He nodded. To Priscilla, she scowled. "I can't believe you! Why do you think I'm living under a new name? For fun? Because I got bored? These people are trying to kill the both of us!" Rage shook her body like it never had before—a cold, brutal wrath. She wanted to cast Priscilla into the void in her own heart, keep her prisoner, locked away with nothing but her own anguish, unable to escape the nothingness of revenge.

Steve rushed to the window. "Three cars."

Covering her mouth, Priscilla backed away. "Are you in danger or something? I—if I knew..."

"If you knew? It doesn't matter what you know! You had no damn idea, no right to help some stranger come after me! Un-be-lievable." Liz followed Steve to the kitchenette. She grabbed a knife from the rack by the sink.

"The balcony here." He pointed, opening a window. "We can get on the roof, slide down the flagpole, but we'll have to be quick and time it right."

The door crashed inward, and Priscilla screamed. A gunshot rang out and Liz threw herself through the open window, Steve right behind her. Not giving it a second thought, she leapt from the edge, tempted to shut her eyes for the few feet she had to fly through open air before wrapping her arms around the pole. She hit the ground hard and fell, but Steve landed gracefully, helping her up.

"Car, car!" he said. Two pale blue cars sat at odd angles with the curb; these, she reasoned, were their attackers' cars. She drove the knife into a front tire but didn't have time to slow the second or third.

The duo sprinted to their four-door, Liz taking the wheel as Steve hurled their bags into the back. He climbed in and she sped off, taking a few sharp turns, and disappearing down side streets. Continuous glances in the rear-view told her they were safe, for the time being.

"What direction?"

"Uh." Steve panted. "West. Southish, maybe. Wherever 'out of this place' is."

"Got it." She fought her instincts to stay at the speed limit. Nothing says, 'We are the droids you're looking for' like hurtling down the street, doing seventy in a thirty-five as you weave in and out of traffic. Keeping steady confuses pursuers, assuming they don't know your car.

A few minutes later, they were on Route 36 and cruising toward the Parkway. Liz had a white-knuckle grip on the wheel and Steve was going through new identities, shoving the scraps of their old lives into another easily disposable carton. He had enough sense to be quiet and let her breathe through her anger.

By the time they were enroute to wherever their new home might be, Liz's nostrils had stopped flaring and her chest no longer heaved like it might tear from her body. Steve looked out the window at yet another town fading away, saying goodbye before he'd even said hello.

"Sorry about your friend."

"She isn't my friend." Then, a minute later, she chimed in, softer. "Wasn't...she wasn't my friend."

"I mean...Yeah. You know."

"What?"

"Nothing."

"Spit it out, dude," she sighed, merging into the fast lane.

Eyeing a soccer mom who was busy flipping them off, Steve tried to word himself as carefully as he could without fogging his meaning. No sense in compounding the issue.

"I meant, I'm sorry things got so bad with her. Addicts... they aren't right, you know, mentally. It's a disease. She wouldn't have done that if she wasn't so far gone...but even I can't take everything away. Suffering that comes from inside, not from a memory, I can't fix."

"You think I don't know that? You shared her pain with me, Steve. I felt that. Her pain was your pain was my pain, and I know every detail as to why she decided to do that. That's not an excuse."

"Huh?" He arched his brow.

"Suffering is not a reason to inflict suffering on others. Having it rough doesn't mean you get to be awful and selfish. We choose, Steve, whether we rule our pain or let it rule us. Which is why, when we get somewhere safe, you're giving me my pain back. I'm not going to rely on others to make my life easier."

"You sure?"

"Do I look unsure?" Her eyes were focused on the road ahead, but the flush of her cheeks and resolute grimace told him enough.

"Alright." He nodded. "Mind if I turn on the radio?"

She shook her head. As soon as it clicked on, they heard, "...ots fired at a Long Branch apartment complex, no evidence of occupants. One woman was found on-scene, killed by a gunshot to the abdomen. More details as the story develops."

He hit 'seek' and something quiet and vaguely country drifted through their speakers. They drove on without talking, trees whipping by as the noonday sun made its way toward the horizon. The roads were mercifully clear.

"Sorry about your friend."

Liz shrugged. "I'll miss who she was. Not who she became...In a way, I guess she died a while ago. And if she were alive, she'd still be dead to me."

They drove in silence until they hit the Parkway.

"What's my name?" she asked.

"You want to pick?"

"We're probably going to skip in another month or two anyway. You pick."

Letting out a slow breath, he went through his stack of fake IDs. "Charlotte Rose."

"Ugh, no." She shook her head.

"Danica Leibowitz."

"Is that Jewish?"

"I think so. Maybe Polish."

"Nah. I know nothing about being Jewish, I'd blow our cover."

"Patrice Oliver."

"Jeez, where'd you get these names, the forties?"

"I make do." He feigned being indignant as she cracked a smile.

"Who are you?"

"Wallace Conrad."

"I'm calling you Wall."

"Whatever, Nameless."

"Don't you start with that again."

"How about Louise Hampton?"

"Fine, whatever."

Wall sealed the box containing their old documents and outfitted their wallets with new identities, slipping fresh fake drivers' licenses into the designated clear pouches. They'd have to abandon the car somewhere and either walk or hitchhike to their next destination, or something reasonably close, but that wouldn't be too hard. Finding a motel or a stable apartment, that'd be a problem, but an easily overcome one.

"Wall?" Louise said, looking over.

"Yeah?"

"I..." She shrugged her shoulders back, looking around the empty road as if she might hit an invisible car.

"Feel guilty about Priscilla?" he guessed.

Shaking her head, she returned her gaze to the blacktop. "No. Not even a little. The way I see it, she made her choices, and what happened was the consequence. I mean, she got killed by the same people she ratted us out to. But that's the problem. I feel like I should feel guilty but don't. There was a time in my life that I definitely would've been empathetic, but I'm not." She touched her chin, then looked at her hand, as if expecting blood. "Is that bad?"

Wall rubbed the back of his head. "You don't feel anything over her death?"

"Precisely."

He shrugged. "Honestly, I don't know. People change. Maybe this is another one. But you're not really asking about her, are you?" Louise didn't reply. "You want to know about that...hollow. Inside you. The ache you don't know how to fill. You're thinking you don't feel guilty because you kept yourself together and she didn't. You suffered alone, while she numbed the pain."

"It crossed my mind."

"I'll be blunt. I don't know where that internal strife comes from. I've seen depression, despair, all that, I've seen it before. I can take a little bit. I can numb people. I can't save them. But you…don't seem to need saving."

"Huh. Guess I'll take that as a compliment." She kept her eyes steadfastly on the road. "What's got me thinking is, if I could save her, I don't think I would've…In fact, no. I'd have let her suffer, and that doesn't bother me at all."

Chapter 23

Discord walked through the halls of the Order, well aware of the red footprints she was leaving, and how she was still coated in fresh blood. This improvised crimson paint splashed across her shirt, pants, face, and back, though how she managed to paint her back that way would forever remain the speculation of those who watched her go. The coppery scent of it all emanated from her like perfume.

During her first days in the Order, others routinely ignored and harassed her. Now, she walked the halls like a crimson ghoul, ready to devour anyone foolish enough to cross her. Upon her promotion to Mistress of Agony, a few had continued their old habit of bothering her. Five days later, they returned, starved, bruised, and covered in deep, infected cuts. One lost a leg. Another lost his nose and an eye. Four of them would shake and cry as she passed.

These people need to suffer. They need to see how wrong they are. One day, they'll fall, and I'll rest easy knowing I stopped them.

Still, each ounce of blood spilled weighed on her conscience, and when she'd catch herself laughing hysterically at nothing, or talking aloud to someone who wasn't actually there, she wondered how much longer she could keep up the act.

She knew the Grand Master had been in contact with that Priscilla girl, but didn't know how or why. Discord had made sure all known associates of Chelsea had their phones bugged, so she'd know if the Vessel was on the move. He'd taken her to one location, and it wasn't likely he'd ditch her now. Still, it bothered her that the Grand Master had gotten involved without telling them.

Walking into the Grand Master's office, she found the room empty. She crossed to his desk and saw a manila envelope there, a Post-it reading: HUDSON HOUNDS. Intrigued, she cracked it open and saw a series of red dots marking kidnappings and murders. It didn't take long for her to figure out that someone was placing the people she killed in the Hall of Creation back in their original homes. The 'Hounds' were really the Order of Nyoru.

Swallowing hard, she noticed LEAD AGENT: THEODORE JOTUN.

That son of a…he's…an FBI agent?

She almost began to panic, wondering if the whole Order was a bizarre sting operation, but shook that idea off. He would've arrested everyone months ago. No, this was clearly his own endeavor—one he didn't intend to abandon.

But she bore responsibility for all the bodies the FBI kept finding. If he wanted, he could easily turn the investigation onto her, sending her to jail and 'closing' the case. That meant she'd have to make her plans subtler. If he grew suspicious, she'd never see the outside of her prison cell.

Swallowing the hard lump of concentrated anger in her throat, she knocked on the Grand Master's bedroom door. A few minutes later, he answered, eyes half-shut.

"Just wanted you to know I dealt with the failures. One died. Two are in the Dark Cells, separate, ensuring maximum anguish. I absolved Derek Ja for managing to place a tracking device on the Vessel's car. We believe they're in Philadelphia." With a pause, she added, "Grand Master," and smiled.

"Oh!" he said, straightening up. "Good, you keep on that. I'll deal with the body."

"No, I've got it covered this time. You have a congregation to lead."

Her eyes fell on a picture tacked to the poster board near

his bed. A picture hung there, the eyes obscured by thumbtacks crudely shoved through the film, but the name below read *Chelsea Valenti—No. 23*.

She turned on her heel and walked off, shoes squelching on the floor. There were only two options: the first, dismember the corpses, grind the bodies to pieces, burn them, and scatter the ashes. The Grand Master could no longer be trusted with her best interests.

Discord slipped around like a red mist, barely perceptible as she flitted from hall to hall. The body was easy enough to dispose of, and when she was done, she returned to her room.

Having more authority now, she wasn't questioned when she disappeared, especially if the Grand Master wasn't around. She'd been able to get her hands on a laptop and install a series of programs that would block her IP address and render her untraceable. She could use it in the Order's HQ without their leader knowing.

Option number two held more risk, but also more reward. She'd wanted to bring this puppet show crashing down but going to the police wouldn't work. Not now. He'd swoop in as the FBI and crush her. She needed to work with someone in the Bureau if there was any hope at all of ensuring their 'leader' went to prison for the rest of his miserable life. She wanted to make damn sure he'd rot behind bars.

Accessing the FBI's website was easy enough but didn't provide her with the information she wanted. Employing another program, she ran a trace and soon her computer had a list of all registered FBI agents, how long they'd been employed, what department they worked in, and their email addresses. After doing a little research, she picked the one she felt would be most useful and wrote her message.

Dear Agent Garcia,

Please take seriously every word I write here, as this is the truth in its entirety: Agent Theodore Jotun is the head of the Order of Nyoru, a cult that has been kidnapping and torturing unsuspecting civilians. You are currently investigating this cult, but the files he has here indicate these deaths are being referred to as gang killings by 'The Hudson Hounds.'

To my knowledge, there is no such gang. We are responsible for the deaths.

The Order is currently in pursuit of a young man and woman. I believe Jotun plans to kill them both.

I would appreciate your utmost discretion. Should he find out about this message, he'll likely try to kill me as well.

Contact me at this address if you wish to pursue the matter further. I would appreciate legal absolution for my help—immunity from the many horrible things I've done here—but I don't require it. I know I'll pay penance, too, one way or another.

But, if you do not believe me or want to get involved, I will deal with matters as I see fit.

Regards,
Discord Sonatina, Mistress of Agony

Chapter 24

One week later...

Sometimes, Louise's mind would wander, and she'd find herself thinking about Priscilla. It was hard enough to lose a friend, let alone one who'd died because of you, directly or otherwise. The idea that she might be responsible for her death was ridiculous, given that Louise had nothing to do with the people who showed up at her apartment, and the fact that Priscilla had invited that catastrophe down on herself.

Her old self, Chelsea, would've felt terrible. In some ways, she still did. But as Louise, as Elizabeth, as Nameless, she didn't. All this jumping around, changing identities, fleeing pursuers, all of it left her feeling divided.

Whenever her mind wandered like this, Louise would berate herself. There was no sense in her feeling guilty. She had done everything right. Priscilla violated her trust and put their lives in danger, costing her own in the process. Louise had enough on her mind without worrying about how she could have prevented a friend's death, if Priscilla could still have been called a friend, given her actions. Besides, they couldn't bring her back.

Of more pressing importance was coping with her parents' death. It wasn't as hard to deal with as she remembered it being that night she walked into her kitchen and found a bloodbath instead of a surprise party. She felt an emotional distance, a disconnect that mirrored her treatment of Priscilla: the event had happened, the people involved were gone, and she could either mourn or move on. In the interest of survival, she chose the latter. She reached into the coldness that had lurked in her heart for so long and cherished its numbing grace.

This didn't stop her from shedding the occasional tear while lying awake at night, thinking about their passing and how, indirectly, she was responsible for that as well. It didn't prevent her from waking up in the middle of the night, roused from sleep by dreams that she stood perfectly still as everyone in her life was slaughtered in front of her.

Her dreams were vicious and her sleep tumultuous, but she was proud of herself for tackling her pain head-on instead of relying on Wall to take it away. Besides, she fit right in as one of the employees of the Mütter Museum. Granted, she was a clerk at the gift shop, but another change in appearance kept her vaguely visible position there a secret from those who might walk by with prying eyes. Fortunately, a recent resignation left the museum understaffed, so she'd been able to fill the gap with few questions asked.

This day was an ordinary one, if anything about her new life could, at that point, be called ordinary. She punched in, worked the till (grateful for the fact that her parents made her take a day job when she was still in the early years of her undergraduate career), and would ride her bike from work to their apartment four blocks away once she punched out. Wall was still looking for a job, so he was laying low for the time being.

Her first break from the monotony of her position came when a soft grunt of pain emerged from the doorway between the museum itself and the gift shop. Being a place full of disturbing oddities, the viewing areas were shadowed and mysterious, in keeping with the 'bizarre' theme. The gift shop was very bright, no doubt to make sure the patrons could view prices with ease, so it wasn't uncommon for people to be caught off-guard by the change in illumination. Moving from the light into the darkness was always disorienting.

In time, a young woman made her way to the till. Louise

assumed this was the person who made the sound a moment earlier, as nobody else walked the shop's floor. This person had ghostly white skin and hair, her eyes hidden by dark sunglasses, though her blood red jacket and pants were distinct enough that it took almost all attention away from her unusual pallor.

"Find everything okay? Is there anything I can help you with?" Louise gave her a once-over, admiring her dedication to the color scheme. Normally she would've only asked one question, but her already established routine was thrown off by the woman's appearance.

Giving a faint smile, she nodded to Louise. The way the light fell revealed her crimson irises.

Ah, an albino. That explains it. Explains some of her wardrobe, at least. The covering. Maybe not the colors.

"Oh yes, just fine, thank you. How are you doing today?" The woman had a cloying undertone. Secrets lurked beneath her tongue.

She slid a book onto the counter, as quiet and subtle as a snake coiling up into someone's pant leg, ready to bite. The title read *Human Evolution: A Compendium of Ordinary People with Extraordinary Abilities.* A popular title, so she was told, one covering people such as a man who could conduct electricity, or another able to light fires with his chi. A slight smirk arced across the pale woman's lips.

Louise shrugged this off and rang her up. "I'm well, thanks. And yourself?"

"Pretty good," she nodded. "Meeting up with an old friend later; wanted to stop by first, take a look around."

"There's a lot of interesting stuff in there, huh? Your total is twenty-four ninety-five."

Handing over two twenties, she maintained the closest thing she could manage to eye contact through her shades. "Do you accept tips?"

"We sure do." Louise nodded to a tip jar. She handed back change and a receipt.

"Oh good," the woman said, dropping fifteen dollars and five cents into the jar. Picking up the book, she waved the hand holding it so the title faced Louise, as if mocking her.

"Have a nice day." Louise was getting more uncomfortable by the minute.

As she slinked toward the exit, Louise noticed the blood-red braid hanging down past her waist and shivered. The woman smiled and said, "You, too, Chelsea."

Her heart clenched, sending a bang through her chest like a car backfiring on a crowded street. Questions raced through her mind, lightning bolts crackling down her neural pathways as she tried to convince herself she'd misheard the woman, but 'Louise' was hard to confuse with 'Chelsea.'

What the hell? We were careful, weren't we? Is she after him or me? And why reveal herself, why let me know she knows who I am?

Grabbing her backpack from the ground by her feet, she vaulted over the counter, pulled out her phone, and punched in Wall's number. The woman was disappearing through the front door.

"Come on, come on, answer!" No response. As she feared, he didn't pick up, his voicemail giving a generic company greeting as Chelsea shoved through the front doors.

In the background, she could hear her manager calling out for her to wait, but she didn't have time to listen to him. Besides, what would it matter if she got fired? She didn't have a resume to worry about. Louise only survived a week anyway.

The stranger slid into the passenger seat of a car waiting by the curb and shut the door, smiling and waving as the car drove off. Sprinting to the side of the building, she tore the lock off her bike, hopped on, and sped down the street as fast as her legs could propel her. Still, as she approached her apartment, she saw the car idling by another, similar vehicle. Both were dark with four doors and tinted windows. She skidded to a halt, heart racing as two people carried a limp body out the front door, shoving it into the trunk. For the first time in months, she would've been very grateful to see a cop, but there was no trace of any such officer.

Committing the New Jersey plates to memory, she waited until the cars were gone to approach her apartment. As expected, the lock had been smashed open, the wood around the doorknob splintered. Nudging her way in, she took quick, careful glances around, her hand resting on the switchblade tucked in her back pocket, but there didn't seem to be a reason to use it.

A cursory glance around each room showed that their possessions had been untouched, as if they'd simply disappeared, never to return to the apartment again.

She put a pot of coffee on and started charging her laptop. She wasn't tired yet, but she wasn't going to rest until she found him. Opening her laptop, she pulled up the internet and searched through the New Jersey motor vehicle registration records, writing down the owners, makes, and models of each vehicle. A Google search turned up the information that one of the two models had a built-in GPS.

Grinning to herself, she looked up the names of local car rental agencies and started making calls to determine which would give her the cheapest ride, no questions asked, as soon as possible. Trapping the phone between her shoulder and ear with a tilted head, she drank the steaming black coffee, ignoring how it burned her tongue, and jotted down details.

She managed to track both the cars and Wall's phone—both signals moving together toward the same location. According to her laptop, the cars were traveling east, heading toward the northern part of New Jersey. It didn't matter where they were going though. New Jersey, New York, Atlantis, wherever it was, she would follow them. Remarking to herself that she was right when she told Wallace to take the offensive against them, she grabbed what remained of her belongings and shoved them in a travel bag. If anyone asked, she was going on a road trip. It wasn't necessarily untrue.

Once her battery charged and her coffee cup emptied, she shut the laptop and shoved it in her backpack, heaving the travel bag over her shoulder. Storming out through the front door, Chelsea left the bike behind; it would've looked suspicious taking one to the rental agency only to leave it there.

She felt a vicious darkness growing inside her. It was more than the fear of losing Wallace and the protection he offered from the Ghost. It was more than feeling protective and wanting to rescue a dear friend.

That black hole in her had always been empty, and she'd tried to fill it on her own, but now, it was hungry. She wanted to throttle them, to watch them scream for mercy as she burned their lives to the ground, to rip the joy from their lives until they had no option but to kill themselves—and she wouldn't let them. The void that once threatened to consume her as a child inverted. Whatever her name was now, she'd only be contented by their absolute, abject, and incomparable misery.

The rental agency was bright and cheery, so her black mood clashed with the décor. She managed to stifle her anger long enough to not alarm the receptionist. Fortunately, this one didn't require a credit card on file. She handed over a wad of cash and slid behind the wheel of an SUV moments later.

Turning the key, she savored the mighty rumble of the engine as it shook the car, as if it shared her fury. She opened the laptop again, eyes focused on the blip of the car that took Wallace. Tracing their route out of town, she mapped the fastest way to follow them.

Growling to a car full of ghosts, she spoke. "I don't care how clever you people think you are. There's no escaping me."

Chapter 25

"Agent Jotun, please see the director immediately." Tommy's voice was so thick with disdain that it practically fell from the receiver as a nauseating sludge. The veteran agent rolled his eyes, wondering what the director wanted to see him for. If it was urgent, they would have contacted him on his cell phone, but this message was on his desk phone.

Like I don't have enough going on without having to deal with these simpletons. They toil and struggle and flop in the mud like the rest of the human animals we serve, pretending to make a difference in the world, never once reforming the criminals. Their methods are reactive, not proactive, only helping those already hurt or dead. When I am the Saint, I will reform this broken system, and those who defy me will suffer in a mental prison more vicious than any physical one.

He hung up the receiver with a grimace, prompting Agent Garcia to look over with raised eyebrows. "Something going on?" she said, her tone suspicious and probing.

"Not that I know of. The director wants to see me. I suppose it's about the Hounds case." He stood up, bracing his hands against his hips as he twisted his upper body. A series of audible pops came from his hips. Garcia looked away, visibly disgusted.

"If it were about that case," she said, picking up her coffee cup, "wouldn't she want to speak to both of us?" A wary eye trailed up and down Jotun's body, as if looking for some giveaway, a microscopic piece of evidence to verify that her partner was not all he claimed to be.

Ignoring her, he shrugged. "How should I know what she thinks? I do know we had a dead-end. We haven't had a lead in weeks. Rumors and speculation do not make for an FBI investigation."

Turning to her computer, she pulled up her emails, not bothering to look at him. "You're right, rumors can't sustain a case, but they sure as hell can start one, and those bodies didn't show up by accident. Someone out there is killing people, and whether this is a gang, a cult, or a bunch of messed-up kids, I intend to find out who's responsible."

He knew better than to argue, so he nodded and walked off to the administrative wing.

She'll go first. Agent Garcia, nosy little wretch. I've languished under her scrutiny for too long. How dare she oppose me?

The hallway seemed emptier than usual. It was always empty, but today it seemed somehow desolate, absence surrounding and choking him the way crowds smother an agoraphobe.

Entering the entry room, Jotun glanced over at Tommy. "Is the director available?"

"I believe so," he said, without his usual attitude. "I'll let her know you're here."

He punched an intercom and announced the agent's presence. Moments later, the director invited him in, asking him to take a seat. He was a child again, perched on his father's knee as the man spoke in his ear, saying, *"Theo, men are strong. You better be strong, boy. If you're not strong, you're not a man, and I'm not raising a woman."*

"Yes, director?" he said, his gaze locking on her cold, blue eyes.

"Agent Jotun," she started, glancing down at some papers on her desk. "As you know, we value your presence at the bureau…"

What the hell is she saying? Am I fired? No, no, like hell am I getting fired! He could feel his pulse rising.

"…But, given the lack of progress, we've opted to make Agent Garcia lead on the Hounds case. You're being reassigned to lead the Ghost case."

Letting out a slow breath, he calmed himself. He could still manipulate Garcia, steer the investigation into the ground—or pin it all on his Mistress. "I can put in more hours, really crack down on this case, director."

She shook her head. "The change is already made; paper-work's been sent through. Things happen, agents hit slumps and dead ends. Investigations need fresh blood, is all. And if we don't up our numbers, someone's gonna get dropped to desk duty. No one wants that."

Fresh blood brought a familiar ache back to the front of his attention. Chelsea was still at large, and he wasn't sure how much longer he could wait. At least he'd oversee *that* case. "I understand," he said, nodding and looking away, pretending to be professional and accept the change while, internally, he wanted to beat her to death with her computer monitor.

"I know it's not easy being pulled, happened to me enough back when I was coming up. Things will work better this way. We can't keep wasting resources checking out the same ex-hausted leads."

"Got it," he sighed. "How do you plan on catching them, then? I assume you've got some idea, otherwise I wouldn't be getting axed."

Frowning at him, she said, "That's up to the new lead. I expect you'll turn over your files to Garcia?"

Garcia. Of course, *of course* she knew about this ahead of time. Why else would she make that snippy 'both of us' quip?

"Yes, director. Of course. And I'll get the files for the Ghost…?"

"Imminently. I instructed Agent Blackstone to leave the file on your desk."

"He doesn't mind?"

"Most people don't mind retirement."

Jotun chuckled. "I see."

"Good." She smiled. "That'll be all."

Rising from his chair, he made his way back down the hallway and to Garcia's desk. "You knew about this, huh?"

She looked up without tilting her head. "I suggested she call you in, tell us both at the same time, but we couldn't reach you."

"Whatever, Garcia." Returning to his chair in a huff, he noticed the Ghost file on his desk.

"You're gonna turn over the Hound file, right?" They both knew it wasn't really a question.

"Yeah, yeah. You'll have it soon."

He opened the manila envelope, looking at what Blackstone had gathered on him. The file contained little outside of victim information and speculation. A photograph of a healthy young woman would accompany one of her corpses, both papers clipped to an investigator's report and a coroner's report.

Except for the last one.

The smiling face of Chelsea Valenti defied him, her rosy cheeks full of blood he couldn't wait to spill. His hands shook with anger as he picked up the officer's report of her parents' deaths. Theo could still feel her father's blood spilling over his hands. His ears rang with the rapport of his silenced 9mm pistol, the sound seeming so powerful, so thunderous back when it foretold his next target's death, no matter how quiet it was.

Now, she was a phantom, as much a ghost as her parents, disappearing from town to town with the Vessel. She was the missing detail, the one loose end he hadn't cleaned up, a stray thread that could unravel his tightly woven world.

Chelsea Valenti, he thought. *Where are you, Chelsea?*

Chapter 26

Killing the engine, Chelsea coasted the remaining way on neutral. The path had been slightly downhill—enough so that she could twist the wheel and silently drift toward the building shown on her laptop. A blinking red blip hovered over this spot on the map, not that the building had an address. It was squat and stone, gray, nondescript walls sitting complacently in the forest, as if to say, *Why bother coming in? You know there's nothing for you here.*

Except this ruse wasn't going to fool her. The cars she'd seen were outside, devoid of passengers. Wallace and the Pale Woman were inside somewhere. Judging by the number of cars off to the side (a quick estimate racked up about two dozen, at least), this building had far more floors below ground than above.

An additional, smaller building sat off to the side, a chain clearly padlocked around the handle. Intuition told her this wasn't the one holding her friend. Refocusing her attention on the main structure, Chelsea crept forward, feet crunching down on small twigs. The sun was blocked by a canopy of leaves, a sight she'd ordinarily have found beautiful. At that moment, all she could think about was how her life had been cast into darkness.

Edging the door open, she glanced around, switchblade in hand. It probably wouldn't have done much to help her, and she knew that, but having a weapon made her feel less power-less, even if she didn't really know how to use it. Most people wouldn't want to piss off an armed stranger. There was a good chance the people who'd taken him were armed as well, but she'd have to take that risk and hope she caught them off guard.

The 'lobby' area was empty, full of scattered paper and debris. It was an almost-convincing image of an abandoned building. There was dirt all over, but not in the center of the room, as if someone or some group knew they'd be walking through a lot and didn't want to get dirty feet.

A defunct-looking elevator sat next to a set of stairs that led down into a darkened stairwell. She reasoned these people used the elevator alone, given that most wouldn't expect it to work, and most wouldn't wander down a pitch-black staircase. Not wanting to risk giving away her element of surprise, she approached the steps and started making her way down.

After the first landing, blackness surrounded her. It was the sort of smothering, claustrophobic blackness that could consume one's rationality, inciting fear, panic, or outright chaos. How many movies had she seen where the lights go out and everyone decides to freak out? How many 'brave heroes' had wandered down into dank cellars and shrieked like a little girl at the sound of a door closing, or a book falling from a shelf?

Careful, she hushed herself. *Stay quiet. They don't know you're here. They'd use a light to navigate this passage if they were going to use it at all. So, one step at a time, keep marching forward.*

Feeling her way, she put her foot down, moving slowly through the dark. She wanted to go faster, and her fear that her friend was being hurt or killed made the blood roar in her ears, but it wouldn't help anyone if she tripped and broke an ankle or alerted his abductors to her presence. Foot by foot, she descended into the earth, feeling all the while like she walked into her own grave.

The darkness gave way to a faint light, one that allowed her to see the outlines of the steps and easily drop down to the final landing. Beyond the doorway was a hallway that branched out in three directions. From the right she heard the whine of a television, a late-afternoon newscast almost overshadowing two people talking. Sidling along the wall, she willed her heart to beat slower and focused her breathing, eavesdropping on the conversation.

"I always thought the Vessel would be more spectacular looking, ya know? Like real big, muscular, handsome. This guy's some beanpole, like he don't eat enough." The first man sounded like a violin being played by a child, all screeching and high-pitched. Chelsea had to resist the temptation to clap her hands over her ears.

"Who cares?" the second said, his deep voice booming like a far-off landslide. "He's just the Vessel, remember? Nyoru will be greater than you can imagine."

"You think? I mean, the tome doesn't say what Nyoru looks like."

"No religion knows for sure what its god looks like, not until that god comes to live on our Earth. It's like when people argue what Jesus looked like. Who cares about how he *used* to look? The second coming and all is what they should worry about. Not that I believe in Jesus, I'm just saying, you know, who gives a crap?"

Chelsea poked her head around the corner and saw the two men standing with their backs to her. They were dressed in street clothes, one in jeans and one in sweatpants. She pulled her head back, tapping her chin with her finger. *No uniforms.*

"So does the Grand Master know who Nyoru is?"

"The Mistress says they don't know, but I bet it's the Master himself. I mean, why try so hard to find the Vessel if he wasn't? My guess is, if Nyoru was out there walking around, it would already have found the Vessel and taken its power back. Kinda makes me worry he won't tell us that's his thoughts, though. So, you know, I hope I'm wrong, because if he's not tellin' us, I imagine he's got something terrible planned for us after."

"Excuse me." Chelsea rounded the corner, looking at the

chatterboxes. "I have orders to transport the Vessel. Could you direct me to his location?"

The two men looked at each other, shrugged, and Deep Voice said, "You new here?"

"No," she scoffed, feigning offense. "I've been working with the Mistress. She needed an attendant so I'm keeping her affairs in order. These orders come from her."

Squeaky said, "Yeah, but I don't recognize ya."

"Look, I was above ground, gathering intel, but if you want to piss me off, I'll tell the Mistress that I can't carry out my orders because you two slugs wanted to badger me."

Turning a sickly green, Deep Voice said, "He's three floors down, at the end of the really long hallway. You can't miss it."

"Yeah, yeah, near the Master's room," Squeaky added.

"Thank you." She gave a curt smile and left. Once in the hallway, she grinned to herself and walked on, keeping her strides quick and steady so those she came across wouldn't think she was doing anything out of the ordinary.

Out of the ordinary for these people, at least.

She'd gambled on this self-aggrandizing 'Grand Master' being so arrogant that the only people here who'd recognize her were him, the albino, and the two who'd confronted them at the cabin. Otherwise, if she assessed right, no one would have any knowledge of what she looked like. From the sounds of things, they'd been focusing so much on the Vessel that they weren't likely to have bothered with her. She prayed she wouldn't run into the two who'd seen her.

She slipped through a few hallways and down a much brighter stairwell, eventually coming to the floor the men had mentioned. Nodding politely to some people milling about a kitchen area, Chelsea wandered until she found "the really long hallway." As she walked toward the door at the end, the pale woman in crimson clothes walked out of another, eyes on the floor.

Her heart stopped from the moment she saw her to the

moment she ducked into a nearby office. It was well-furnished with an oak desk in the center, books along the wall, and a computer. Back to the door, Chelsea listened for footsteps but heard none. But the light coming under the door flickered as someone walked past.

She quickly realized she was in the Grand Master's office but didn't have time to look around. Creeping back into the hallway, she quickly padded along to the end, approaching the heavy black door. Pulling it open, she slipped in and quietly shut it.

The Vessel sat in the center of an empty room, hands tied behind his back, a blindfold over his face. He shook like a strong wind was trying to blow him away. Darting forward, Chelsea pulled the rag off his face and was struck with full force by a blast from his mirrored eyes.

Writhing on the dirty floor, she bit down on her lip, eyes shut tight against the pain. Months of starvation and daily beatings had reduced someone's will and bones to pulp, and she felt every excruciating blow, each accompanied by a hiss of, *You failure*, or, *How dare you act so shamelessly? Nyoru would destroy you.*

There was too much going on to let this onslaught stop her. Besides, the pain had already begun to fade. She'd gotten used to the pain he shared, and neither the severity nor the surprise stunned her long. Pulling herself up, she ignored the jerks and spasms as her body 'remembered' the blows 'she'd' sustained. A few tears ran down her face as beads of blood ran from the Vessel's eyes. Upon recognizing her, he let out a groan.

"What are you doing here?" he whispered.

"Rescuing you, duh," she hissed back. "What's wrong with your eyes?" Her fumbling hands tried to untie the rope holding his hands together despite the flash of a boot stomping down and breaking her fingers. Fire raced through her veins, from her hand to her neck, radiating, but she grimaced and worked around the phantom sensations.

"I'm sorry, I...I overloaded. If I take on too much, that... That can happen. Look at me, I'll take it back."

As the memory played out, she adapted to the pain and finished untying him. "The hell you will. We need to get out of here before you worry about any of that."

"Look, just...Humor me, you don't deserve—"

"If you keep this up, we're going to get caught, and life is going to get a whole lot worse for everyone, so be quiet."

He snapped his jaw shut and followed her lead. They walked into the empty hallway, but the Vessel tapped her shoulder, motioning to the Grand Master's room. Stepping inside, he said, "There's a back way out, a service exit. The key should be in here."

"Let's get looking, then."

The Vessel searched over the bookshelves while Chelsea took a seat at the desk, examining the drawers. She felt drawn to one and came across a leather-bound book. On the cover read the words *The Saint of Glorious Pain.*

"What's this?" Her mind continued to play out the illusionary beatings, but she no longer felt them, or minded the starvation and solitude.

The Vessel walked over and said, "Their guidebook, of sorts. Has all their rituals and myths and proverbs and other nonsense."

She nodded, almost returning it, but didn't. Taking it would really disrupt their operations. Besides, she wanted to see what it said. Holding onto it, she looked at the other material on the desk while the Vessel went back to searching for the key out.

Chelsea stumbled across a manila folder. Opening it revealed the Hudson Hounds case, complete with the words LEAD AGENT: THEODORE JOTUN.

"Son of a..." she mumbled. *An FBI agent? No wonder he hasn't been caught.*

The Vessel glanced over but didn't react. She crossed to another door, entering what looked like a small bedroom with poster board along a wall. Chelsea's jaw dropped as she looked over a collage made of images of her, of her parents, of the various places they'd been and names she had assumed. This man had been watching *her*, not just the Vessel.

"What? He's after the both of us?" she whispered.

The Vessel approached, looking over the images. "God-damn."

"You were right all along." Chelsea shook her head. "Teaming up made it easier for him to get what he wanted."

"Maybe."

"Maybe?" She looked over at him.

"Sucked doing all this alone. Sucks a lot less with you. And I got caught when I was all alone. I'm glad you insisted we skip out of town together. I'd probably be dead or worse right now if you weren't there to rescue me."

Chelsea snorted. "Don't worry, I'll try not to hold that over you."

They stared into the Grand Master's bedroom for a moment longer. Chelsea walked in, more resentful with each step, and tore the collage down, crumpling the papers and shoving them in her pocket. She'd destroy them later. Make it that much easier to evade him—not that he couldn't just print the papers out again. Still, she wanted him to know she'd been here. That she'd walked right into his bedroom and slipped away, perfectly unharmed.

The Vessel nodded to her, stepping back as they turned to leave, except they couldn't, because someone was leaning against the door, staring at them.

"Did you two find what you were looking for?"

Part Four: Empty Souls

Chapter 27

"You sure about this?" Chelsea looked back at Discord. They stood above ground, by the car Chelsea had rented, having taken the rear exit. The albino, as always, had her sunglasses on, their lenses dark enough to disable the Vessel's ability to inflict or take pain. He couldn't do a thing if he couldn't make eye contact.

They hadn't gotten much time to talk, but they'd exchanged the important information. Who the Grand Master was, why he wanted each of them, his 'ultimate goal' of becoming 'the Saint.' During his brief captivity, the Vessel showed enough of his power that Discord no longer doubted that *The Black Tome* held some merit, but still didn't regard the cult's leader as a soon-to-be god.

"I'm sure. Leave, now. And take this." She passed them both pieces of paper with a phone number and an email account. "My information. Message me as soon as you're safe. When Agent Garcia knows more, I'll pass the information along. Until then, it's important he thinks you escaped again. Otherwise, he'll never be sentenced for what he's done."

"Wait, Talia Garcia?" Chelsea interrupted.

Discord's thin eyebrow curved up over the rim of her sunglasses. "Yes. You know her?"

"Her sister, Jordan. I know her sister. Knew, I guess. Long time ago. It's good though. She keeps on top of things. She'll make sure Jotun is found guilty."

"What about you?" the Vessel said, glancing at the road.

"You're guilty here, too."

She shrugged. "I'm of no consequence. Go. He'll be here soon."

"We won't forget this." Chelsea slid into the passenger's seat. Moments later, they'd departed, a thin plume of dust rising in their wake. Discord returned to the main building, checking her phone.

On the way back, looking forward to seeing the Vessel again.

Smirking, she put her phone away. *Tough luck, Theo.*

It had been difficult for her to admit the Order was right about the Vessel's powers. It made her wonder what else they were right about, but she wasn't going to cater to their violence any more than she had to. Assuming their god was real, she prayed it'd have mercy on her for betraying its beloved cult. Though she'd had the opportunity, she wouldn't make eye contact with the Vessel; breaking apart on her own was preferable to inflicting the misery of torturing dozens of people on someone else.

As far as the others knew, the Vessel was still downstairs, so she walked down to the now-empty holding cell and returned to the higher floors, pretending to have just discovered his absence. She gathered everyone in the chapel.

"Do you mind explaining," she growled, silencing the room, "why the Vessel is once again missing?"

A low murmur spread through the crowd. People exchanged eye contact but refused to speak up.

"We had a plan. A good, simple plan. Imbue as much pain as we could into him in preparation for Nyoru's return to our plane and NOT to let him escape. Who's the genius who screwed that one up?"

There was another series of nervous shuffles. She frowned. Her sinister reputation was getting in the way. Rather than obeying her command, they now cowered at the prospect of her wrath.

She relented, massaging the bridge of her nose. "Finding the Vessel is more important than punishing those who allowed him to slip away in the first place. Confession will suffice. If I have to find out on my own who was responsible, then I will be very disappointed with your lack of cooperation. If such disappointment comes to pass, then rest assured there will be no hope of mercy. Or," she added, glaring down at the mass of frightened faces, "absolution."

A tall man with a scruffy beard and a deep voice looked at the man next to him and stood up. "Yeah, him, I didn't do it, but there was this one girl, didn't recognize her. Said she'd been given orders from you to move the Vessel to another room, got all nasty when we started asking questions. Said she would report me to you, so he told her what she wanted to know. If I had known she was lying, I'd have stopped him."

Discord made a mental note to warn Chelsea to change her appearance drastically if, and hopefully when, she opted to get in contact. "Thank you. Did anyone else see this woman?"

The tall man looked down at someone next to him. Shaking his head, the littler of the two glanced up at her and then hid his face.

"You there," she said, pointing at him. "Something you'd like to add?"

The seated man stared at her for a moment, then his eyes rolled back in his head and he hit the floor. Rolling her own eyes, Discord loomed over the trembling masses.

"I assume he was with you when you saw her?"

The tall man nodded, and she instructed him to get his friend out of the room. He dragged the limp body away while she asked if anyone else had information to share. A few others mentioned seeing her walking around on the lower floor, but assumed it was another acolyte they didn't know.

She dismissed the crowd as the Grand Master returned from his day job, shoulders slumped and eyes dark. The crowd parted to let him through, then emptied from the room, leaving them alone.

"Rough day?" Discord gave a faint smile, knowing that however bad his day had been, it was about to get worse.

"It doesn't matter, not anymore. No amount of mundane, trivial inconveniences could spoil the day where I get to see the Vessel and absorb his power. Nothing can spoil this day."

"The Vessel has escaped again...Grand Master."

He fixed his gaze on his Mistress of Agony, simultaneously disbelieving and not at all surprised by the news. "How?"

"That's what I'm trying to determine. He appears to have slipped by us completely undetected, perhaps with the aid of that girl he's been traveling with."

Running his hands through his thinning hair, Theo began to pace. Not only was his victim perpetually escaping him, but she was also thwarting his destiny of becoming Nyoru. The prophecy clearly stated that once awakened, the Saint would live in human flesh, nigh immortal, but it wouldn't matter if Theo were to be imprisoned or killed before that happened. You can't become a god if you're dead, and it was getting harder to keep the rest of the FBI off his trail.

"They will both be dealt with, in time. For now, I am going to my office, and if any member of the order wishes to disturb me, I'll personally oversee their punishment."

"As you wish, Grand Master. I'll alert the others that they're not to bother you. Should there be any developments in our pursuit of the Vessel, you will be notified immediately."

Thanking her, Theo returned to his combination of office and bedroom, taking his seat at his desk. Were his grandfather still alive, he would've been barking to get up, to get on his feet and go find those who had betrayed him, those who would make him wait and suffer instead of becoming what he was destined to be.

Opening the top drawer, he reached for *The Black Tome*. The book was gone.

Chapter 28

"The Vessel carries with him or her the power of Nyoru, the Saint of Glorious Pain. It is the Vessel's duty as bearer of this sacred gift to use it and allow it to mature, to develop it and strengthen it, so that when the Vessel comes into contact with the Incarnate, the former can share the power in full.

"Upon transference, both the Vessel and Nyoru will be in possession of this power. The Vessel's continued survival will be contingent on the will of the Saint. Since they would both wield the holy power, if Nyoru wishes it, the Vessel will be executed immediately.

"Being human, the Vessel is not capable of fully wielding this ability, having a limited capacity to store pain, and upon taking in too much, or being surprised, frightened, or threatened, the Vessel may spontaneously expel stored agonies. In such an event, the Vessel will physically suffer, and may bleed from the eyes or lose sight entirely. Nyoru is immune to such deleterious effects, as this power stems from on high and the Saint is therefore fit to use it as desired.

"Should the Vessel be killed or lose the power before transferring it to Nyoru, a new Vessel will be formed, and the duty to see the power used to maturity will fall to that person instead."

Glancing up at Mark, who had selected a new identity once they were safely away from the Order's compound, Skyler widened her eyes dramatically.

"This is some messed-up garbage."

"How elegant." Mark parked the car. Since they were driving a rental, it had to be returned to a rental agency. To make sure the Order didn't pick up on their trail too easily, they'd driven southwest, planning to hop on the nearest northbound bus and ride it until they found themselves in any major city where they could vanish.

Frowning, she went inside, returning the key and flashing her 'Louise' driver's license. They'd destroy it as soon as they were able, but for now they needed to make sure there was no reason to raise suspicions. Smiling cheerfully, the receptionist noticed nothing.

Walking back outside, Skyler looked over at Mark. "Your eyes okay?" He chuckled, brushing her off, but she stopped him. "Seriously, you were bleeding pretty bad before, and the book said you could go blind."

"Yes, I'm fine!" He tried to assuage her fears. "And don't tell me you believe everything that book says. That's how cults get started."

Marching up beside him, she said, "Of course I don't believe everything some idiot decided to write down. You know how many times this was probably rewritten? Even if it is the word of some god, humans put it to paper. Humans are no more capable of understanding the wills of gods than the rocks are of understanding quantum physics. All I know is that you fired off without warning several times, and every time you did, I saw blood running down your cheeks. You've been bleeding more lately, so stop acting so high and mighty, Vessel."

She felt her stomach drop out from beneath her as she said it. Mark looked back, his own pain in his eyes, then watery and distant. They walked on in silence. Soon enough, they came across a bus stop, and one showed up with NEW YORK glowing above the windshield. They trudged onto the bus, paying their fare as the bleary-eyed, paunchy driver pretended to care about who was coming on board. Aside from them, there were only two other riders on the bus.

Taking a seat in the back, Skyler crossed her legs, fidgeting with the travel bag she placed in her lap. Mark pointedly stared out a window, avoiding any accidental chance of gazing her way. The silence between them was thick and uncomfortable, like a wool blanket in August.

"Mark, I…" she whispered, trying to get his attention without others overhearing. He didn't seem to want to listen, so she backed off, letting him cool off. Twenty minutes passed before she tried again. "I shouldn't have said that. Sorry." She looked down. "You're…important to me. Not romantically or anything, just…I know we're supposed to know each other. I want to make sure you're okay."

Sighing, he leaned back in his seat. "How are you dealing with that…stuff?"

"The parent thing? Or the thing from before?" They almost met each other's gaze but didn't. "Either way, fine. Doesn't bother me much now."

"You sure? I can…You know."

"Yeah, I'm sure. How are you holding up? Still…too much?"

His lips thinned to a white line. "I'll manage."

"Let me know if you can't."

The bus jostled along toward New York, New York. Some trees would go by, but mostly it was a landscape of graffiti-tagged underpasses, abandoned office buildings, and smog-belching factories. New Jersey was the Garden State, alright—weeds bloomed in cracked concrete as ivy tried to take back buildings, crawling along the walls, trying to tear them down one vine at a time.

They neared a tunnel to New York when he said, "What did you mean, let you know?"

"I mean…I can handle more if you can't. I don't want you to suffer."

"Nor I you."

"Let me help a little bit. Take the edge off. We can suffer together."

He looked over. "You sure?"

Skyler nodded. She'd never been more sure of anything.

Mark locked eyes, his becoming mirror-like again as she experienced the acute sensation of someone cutting her with a power saw. Pinky, ring, middle, index, thumb, then the hand, severed at the wrist, ensuring maximum pain as a tourniquet wrapped around her upper bicep, stemming the blood. Staring down at her hand, she was struck by the sensation of becoming a cripple, then it faded away, the pain stored in a memory bank in the dark parts of her heart. She barely felt that coldness now, the one that haunted her through her earlier years. If anything, Skyler embraced the way she numbed to pain now.

"You okay?" He arched his brow.

She nodded. "Are you?"

Mark gave a slow, weary smile. "Better now."

The bus stopped and they climbed off. Night had fallen, but the streets were, of course, still busy. New York City rarely slept. When it did, other parts came alive. They'd be two leaves lost among many, many forests.

"It'll be easy to hide here, huh?" His gaze surveyed a fleet of cabs, each crammed full of people, yet doing nothing to thin the throngs on the sidewalk.

Skyler grinned at the lights all around them. "Precisely."

Chapter 29

Four Months Later...

Hello Director,

I wanted to let you know that a couple people have come forward in the Hounds case. I was right: they admitted to being part of a cult that would abduct and torture people, saying that they needed to "show the world the value of pain." Some crap about transferring power to an ancient god. Anyway, they are compiling sketches of their former leader now. They don't know the name of the man who was leading the group, but they know what he looked like. It's not much, but it's a start.

Sincerely,
Talia Garcia

Theo shut his laptop with a snarl. He'd hacked Garcia's email account to keep tabs on how close she was getting. Getting up to pace his tiny living room, he poured himself a drink and ignored the fact that it was only eleven in the morning. He had grown suspicious of Discord three months ago and spent the weeks since carefully stalking and subtly interrogating her, along with tapping her communications. She thought he didn't know about her laptop. Idiot.

"It's bad enough that backstabbing traitor screwed me," he muttered, "but there's no way I'm letting this whole damn thing fall apart. I have worked too hard. I will not be brought down by some *mortals.*"

Garcia was relentless. Every time he turned around, he was hearing a new rumor about what she did, about new witnesses interrogated, new bodies found, new evidence analyzed, about traces of toxins that required a high security clearance, or really good black-market connections, to obtain. She was closing in on him, and without the Order, he was at a serious disadvantage.

He'd been able to track his targets to a car rental agency in a town whose name he couldn't be bothered to remember. It wasn't important anymore. After that, the trail vanished. He assumed they paid cash for everything, but three separate bus lines led out to three separate directions. They could've gone north, west, or south, and if he guessed wrong, he'd be looking for a very long time.

The only clue he had was that, much like Theo himself, the Vessel was good at considering every angle and was paranoid as a result. He never visited the same location twice. Breaking that rule was how they almost caught him at the cabin, so he wasn't likely to visit a repeat location again, no matter how big the city. The south line stopped in Long Branch. The west line, Philadelphia. That left the north line: New York.

The Vessel had been there once, for a while, as a kid, but not since fleeing from town to town, attempting to escape his fate. Theo was also betting on him having no knowledge of the Order's disbandment.

After the Vessel slipped from their grasp while captured in their own headquarters, taking *The Black Tome* with him, Discord had decided to reveal her real intentions. Slowly and quietly, over the coming weeks, she began manipulating the other members, convincing them that Theo was a liar and a con artist, with his lack of leadership due to his growing alcoholism, losing the Tome, and "giving orders that led to the Vessel's escape."

She was able to win over enough members that, when they departed, their ranks were too thin to continue. The remaining members decided to abandon the Order of Nyoru as well.

Theo was on his own, leading an FBI investigation into his own serial killing tendencies, desperately trying to prove himself a god in an atheist world.

He looked back at the computer screen. There wasn't much he could do to improve his situation, but what little he could do, he would. It was time to go after the Vessel himself, and he'd start by visiting Garcia.

Chapter 30

Skyler had read *The Black Tome* cover to cover and, as she expected, it was mostly nonsense. The book was nothing more than a compendium of every cult cliché in Hollywood: the world was coming to an end, and only the faithful would be shown mercy; their god was a just but vicious god who would punish non-believers and dissidents; and, of course, all famous figures were men. The Vessel, the Incarnate, and Nyoru, were almost constantly referred to as He, as if the writers had been sitting around with their frat buddies chanting "Bros before Hoes."

She'd been tempted to burn the whole thing, but instead tore out the ritual sections, the end of days myth, and some passing details about the Vessel, taping the important-seeming pages to a wall of her room. Apparently, since it had never happened and Nyoru "could not impart such sacred knowledge to mankind," no one really knew how the transference was supposed to work.

One issue she had was that both parties could keep their abilities, assuming Nyoru didn't kill the Vessel. In a fit of aggravation, she crossed out all iterations of 'transference' since the power was being copied, not transferred, and that misuse drove her crazy. The pages were adorned by her red scribbles and, "F. SEE ME AFTER CLASS," on the top one.

Mark had shared some of the more painful memories he'd picked up along the way, all of which she sublimated into her emotional void while he found suitable targets. Once he did, he emptied out what pain he'd picked up, at her insistence, only taking enough back to 'punish' someone who deserved a little extra suffering. She liked this process—sharing the pain. The more she saw into other peoples' hearts, the more in-tune she felt with how the world was supposed to work.

Halloween was three weeks away and, given that they'd made a career out of hiding their identities, Skyler couldn't resist getting into the holiday spirit and making a run to a local costume store. Mark had rolled his eyes but didn't object.

After some deliberation, she picked an 'Invisible Man' costume for Mark and an 'Unknowable Creature' costume for her, which came with makeup and a mask, making it look like she had no face at all, beyond her eyes. She liked the faceless aspect, just two eyeballs floating in an empty sea. It also didn't have 'sexy' cutouts, which would've annoyed her.

When he came back from his shift working the bar at a nearby dive, Mark was in no way prepared to see Skyler in all white, appearing to float thanks to the raised heels on her boots and an excessively long dress. She'd grown used to his pain potshots, but not for this particular memory. She'd seen addiction, abandonment, abuse, war crimes, prisons, but never Mark's own past. This time, when that deep blue tunnel closed in around them, it didn't feel cold. If anything, it was a blast of heat, scorching her with its intensity, a physical pain driving deep into her skull.

The sensation only lasted until the memory took full effect. Unlike others, which were almost always connected, or even caused by, a physical pain—torture, starvation, beatings, drug cravings—this was unfettered grief. This was a depression so deeply rooted that there was no escaping it. Covering her eyes, Skyler felt this misery overlaid by helplessness—the need to help, the failure to do so, an aching sadness that grew more intense with every tear that rolled down her face, both the depression and the feeling of worthlessness amplifying until threatened to rip her apart. She felt him desperately trying to save someone who couldn't be saved—someone who didn't even want to try to escape the hole of her depression. The neurons in Skyler's brain began to misfire and the world around her became a flurry of sparks and colors disconnected from reality.

Mark put his hand under her chin, tilting her head up and attempting to lock eyes with her, but the idea of him trying to take this back, of having hidden something so intense and so deep for so long, infuriated her. He made the connection, but she broke it, shattering the blue tunnel and slapping him across the face.

He drew back, palm to his cheek.

"What...What is this?" She raised a hand to her aching chest. As before, the pain was already fading to nothing but a twinge. A sore spot in her emotional makeup. Her head hurt far worse. If he'd literally broken her skull open and rammed a finger into her pineal gland, it probably wouldn't have hurt as bad.

"Give it back and I'll tell you." He tried to take a commanding stance, but his voice shook.

"No." Skyler shook her head. "I want to feel this as you feel it. I want to understand this pain as you tell me the story, because I have a feeling this isn't new. This is a pain you've been living with your whole life, isn't it? That's why it hurts so much."

It looked as though he was going to try to lock eyes with her again but thought better of it. "Yeah, it is." He wiped the trickle of blood off his cheek. The sclera of his eyes were almost entirely crimson.

"Then I suggest you sit down and tell me about it because neither of us are leaving this room until you do." To drive home her point, she crossed to an armchair and sat down, reclining, fingers clasped in front of her. Rather than like a ghost, the flowing white robes made her look like a priestess, waiting in meditation for him to make his offering. Mark tried to take the pain back, but she dismissed the connection again.

Realizing he had no other choice, Mark took a seat on the

couch. Elbows on his knees, chin resting on his raised hands, he tried to find the right words. "You know I've always had this...gift, as some call it. Even as a child. I would go to school, and I would see how my peers suffered, how Maria's parents were getting divorced, how Danny was upset about his broken leg because it meant he couldn't ride his bike with his dad after school, how the art teacher, Ms. Bingham, got stood up, or worse, how her latest one-night stand once again didn't call her back. I wouldn't keep anything from them though. I knew better—knew not to get caught. What I took, I gave right back. But there I was, wanting to help, unable to. I was never able to."

Skyler felt the reverberation of his helplessness in her own chest.

"Never?"

He resisted the temptation to look at her as it would've enticed him to try taking his pain back again.

"I can't fix people. I can fix their problems, but if they have a mental disorder, or if their outlook is so negative that they create their own problems, I only numb things for a while. I could fill myself to breaking with their pain, and not make them any better for it. Some act like...like factories for suffering. I learned that...I learned that when I was still a boy.

"My mother had clinical depression. I kept trying to help her. I kept taking and taking, but she wouldn't get any better. Happier for a while, perhaps. She'd smile for a short time. Then she'd sleep for a week, get up, take a handful of some prescription, and say it wasn't my fault. That I was a good boy for trying to help, but she couldn't be helped. I should've listened."

This explained the abyssal despair, and the self-doubt, the worthlessness, all of which she now regarded factually rather than emotionally. She was aware of pain inside her but didn't feel it, as was often the case when she cut out her emotional side for her analytical one. Anguish became another organ, as present as her heart, but just as insensate.

"She kept saying, 'Don't tell your father, don't tell your

father.' He had a temper. I didn't want him to get angry with me, to tell me I was a failure for not curing her, that this power meant I'm supposed to be some divine being, and my using it poorly was an offense to the god that gave it to me, so I tried in secret. I dealt with all the pain I took from her, not realizing I had a limit. Things got to the point where I didn't sleep, I didn't eat, I was doing poorly at school…I kept taking though. Then…"

"…Then you overloaded," Skyler finished. She saw, from his perspective, a middle-aged brunette reeling backwards, hands over her eyes as all the light of her world went out. Mark dropped his face into his palms. "You couldn't have known that was going to happen."

"I…" he started. Taking a breath, he straightened up, looking over at her. "It doesn't matter whether or not I knew. I took her normal depression and inflicted it back on her probably tenfold. She couldn't handle it. I don't think anyone could have.

"I realized what had happened, but I was a kid, and I was in pain, and my eyes were bleeding. I was scared and I wanted my mom to help me, but she didn't do a thing…Actually, that's wrong. She said, 'It's okay,' and I could hear the sadness in her voice, but as much as I wanted to take it back, all I saw was red when I opened my eyes. I called out to her, trying to wipe the blood away, and then I heard the gunshot."

Despite the normal noise of the New York City streets, the apartment was unusually quiet. All the air forced itself against the windows and doors, blocking outside interference, leaving a near vacuum in which they could talk without being disturbed. Skyler looked at the floor, recognizing that portion of himself that he had kept locked away for so long now radiated in her, humming like a psychic string that, having been plucked, would never again sit quietly.

"Psychologists like to say children cannot comprehend death. This isn't true. Gifted or otherwise, some of my earliest memories are of darkness and fear. The fear that I might die. The fear that those close to me would die. The fear that I wasn't meant to live, or that I'd drive away my family with my...gift.

"Death, I understood, is about absence. It's when 'is' becomes 'was.' When 'we' becomes 'I.' Didn't recognize the sound when I first heard it, but the way it shook me...There wasn't a doubt in my mind about what had happened.

"Crawling at first and then stumbling to my feet, barely able to see, I made my way into my father's study. There was a macabre poetry to the scene: her, in my father's high-back leather chair, a splatter of blood and brain matter across his books, his wall, his map of the United States, pockmarked with pinholes so he would never forget the places he visited for work. All these things that made up who my father used to be, these things that kept him away from us, that kept her stewing in her own misery when he could have been trying to help her, these things were hers now. They would be forever stained by her last act, and every time he stepped inside that room, he'd be reminded of his greatest failure.

"I stared through crimson vision at the hole left in my mother. That was her escape, her exit route, the path by which her soul traveled so she wouldn't have to suffer on this earth any longer. Though the gun was in her hand and her finger on the trigger, it was nothing more than the literal version of the metaphorical bullet that I shot her with. Sinking to my knees, I cried, I cried and cried my own tears instead of hers. For once the pain was fully mine, not someone else's, but it was a hollow and empty moment. One that didn't end until my father came home.

"He stood in the doorway to his study, briefcase in hand, in his nicely pressed suit, as if this were any other day, and stared down at both his wife and his child, soaked and stained with blood. In my grief, I accidentally shot him as well, sharing the full emotional weight of what had happened, but I took this back an instant later. Regardless, my cover was blown, my guilt revealed, and to my surprise, he wasn't angry...I wish he had been. I wish he'd beaten me, screamed at me, taken out a knife and attacked me, but I have found that fate's most interesting plans are not left to coincidence, and I suppose mine is a truly interesting case indeed.

"What I had not known was that my father was in possession of a book, one that his grandfather had meticulously reconstructed, breathing new life into a dilapidated, worn, and forgotten text. Its pages outlined the return of a god, one whose chief power is to take away or inflict untold degrees of pain on those it comes across."

Skyler watched him, not reacting. His memories, alive inside her, already told her all this. She knew from the moment he unleashed his oldest, deepest pain that the Grand Master, Theodore Jotun, also happened to be Mark's father. But Mark needed to face this. Tell this story himself. In recounting, he could confess all he'd been carrying, and find solace in disclosure.

He continued, "This book tells of a vessel that will be born with the god's power, and it must use that power, helping it to grow and mature. Once the ability has fully manifested, it will be shared with that 'Saint,' as they call it. That being, the Incarnate, will walk this earth for untold years. The magnitude of pain it wields is said to strengthen it, giving its form enhanced life, letting it live for centuries, allowing it to be shot, stabbed, even decapitated, but never die.

"I don't know what I believe. I don't know what gods or goddesses are out there, what forces govern our lives, or even what I am, but I know my father viewed me as this thing, the Vessel. He...Once he felt the ebb and flow of pain in his heart, he imagined himself the Incarnate. He formed a cult, the purpose of which was solely to train me until the day when I could transfer my power to him. The members subjected themselves to incredible pain, to starvation, to beatings, burnings, the murder of their own families, all in the prospect that I would then take it away, using my gift as a weapon against people my father deemed to be heretics. All the while, I was only ever called 'the Vessel.'

"For years, I dealt with his insanity, my own mental limits tested by the miseries I suffered. The first chance I got, I fled his compound, stumbling across freeways and state lines. I wandered for days, following the path of a small river, eating a few provisions I stole from the cult. By the time I found anyone to help me, I was half dead from exhaustion, having barely survived. A family was out camping when I stumbled into their area, passing out by a tent.

"When I woke up, I was in hospital. When the staff deemed me fit to answer questions from state authorities and child services, I was asked what my name was." He scoffed, shaking his head. "For all that I've seen through others' eyes, I was surprised I still felt sad for myself when I said I didn't know my own name."

Skyler's heart ached—for him, not because of him.

"They assumed I was confused from exhaustion and malnutrition, but once I was well enough to get back on my feet, I ran away. I knew, in the intuitive way that most children know things, that if I had stayed, I would've been turned into an orphanage, and that my father would once again find me, that I would be brought back to his care. He would pull strings, call in favors…He's a powerful man, and he would've gotten away with it.

"I fled, first the hospital, then the city, then the state, never knowing where his reach extended—never knowing where I could go that would put me at a safe distance. I've hitched rides and lived in Ohio, Montana, Nevada, Texas. I have been dozens of people, but never myself. There has never been time, never been space, never been a chance."

His voice began to shake, and he looked at Skyler with pleading, desperate eyes.

"The only thing that kept me together throughout all this,

the only thing that kept me myself after all the names I've assumed and the pain that I have taken and given, is the weight of my mother's death. The memory and misery have been my only defining characteristic, the only evidence that I was ever once a real person. Whatever I am, it is a product of that moment, so please, let me have it back."

Mark had begun to tremble like the ground before an earthquake. Skyler moved the footrest to her chair, coming to sit in front of him. She took his hands in hers, making eye contact.

"Okay. It's yours. Go on. Have it."

Letting him lock on, she felt the tunnel close in again, and they were a single emotional space, bound together by a single tragedy, the likes of which only they could've stood and still been sane. Then it ended, the piece of his heart returning to him, while she felt nothing but the vague removal of yet another misery, a piece of astral anatomy discarded.

"Thank you," he whispered, shutting his eyes.

Impulsively, she kissed his forehead, as a mother kisses her child to stop them from crying. She knew exactly how he felt, using his loner attitude to keep himself from connecting, afraid of being hurt—or hurting someone else—the way he had when he was a boy.

"To think, all this is because of your own father, targeting me because I looked like your mother." She hadn't studied the other 'Ghost' killings. If she had, maybe she'd have pieced something like that together, realizing that all the victims were roughly the same age and appearance. Or maybe she wouldn't have. It didn't matter now.

Mark shook his head. "He is a sick man with good intentions. I...I have run all these years, never turning him in...Because even if I had evidence, I can't blame him. Coming home to all that...It must've broken him. It's my fault. If I hadn't..."

"Hey." She tapped his forehead to break him out of his thoughts. "Everyone breaks at some point, but we have to pull ourselves together and move on when we do. Pain is not an excuse to cause harm. What your father did is not your responsibility. You'll see that someday. But we have evidence now, and Discord and Agent Garcia are counting on us to lure him out. We'll catch him, Mark. We will. Count on it."

Chapter 31

Agent Garcia let out a sigh and kicked the front door to her house shut. It was late, like it usually was. The director had really been pushing her over the past few months, saying that the investigation was at "a critical juncture," which she knew was administrative talk for, "I really need something to make me look good, so dammit, you're going to get out there and close the case."

She looked through her mail while walking along to her kitchen, listening to the quiet slap of her footsteps on the hardwood floor. Hers was a simple home, one inherited from an uncle who made a modest living as a business owner. She'd helped him out in his shop at least once a week until she graduated from college and entered the FBI, so, having no kids of his own, he saw no more fitting an inheritance than a house that, in essence, she helped pay for. He often said that his business never would've survived without her assistance, but she knew he was an old and lonely man who appreciated their time together. She'd enjoyed the time, too.

The creaks and groans of her house reminded her of him a lot, more so than the picture of him she kept on a table in the hallway, out of respect for his memory and out of respect for the fact that he was the original owner.

Very few houses were owned by the people who originally lived there, but he'd bought an unused tract of land outside of New York City and had a house built on it. He'd been the only owner, and until he died, the only tenant, not including guests.

Garcia's life was not so different. She spent most of it at work and her time off during various side jobs. There was a well-tended garden in the back of her house because of her handiwork, and she read at a youth literacy program once a month. Though they did consume time she might've spent with friends or looking for a love interest, she was young and felt fine knowing that she had years during which to find someone to settle down with.

Flipping on the kitchen light, she crossed to the island in the center of the room, the lights above reflecting off her countertop, which was a slab of brown granite speckled with greens and reds. It reminded her of her garden, when it wasn't strewn with various bits of debris—cooking utensils, mail, things from work, and the like. She was messy by necessity, finding that she worked much better when allowed to bask in chaos.

Throwing down her mail, which was nothing more than spam in the latest issue of *Reader's Digest*, she took a carton of leftover Chinese food from her refrigerator, dumped it on a paper plate, and shoved it in the microwave, absently punching in a minute thirty. While the food cooked, she opened her briefcase, pulling out the composite sketch of the leader of the gang she thought was called the Hudson Hounds.

According to those who turned themselves in, it was really a cult known as the Order of Nyoru, a pagan organization that worshipped some unheard-of god, one that seemed to be in control of pain. She really didn't care what they believed, so long as she wasn't trying to clean up another Jim Jones catastrophe, and though they claimed to have disbanded, she knew better than to assume cultists would calmly and willingly give up their disturbed, delusional ideas. If they'd been off-the-wall enough to hold masses, read from a 'bible,' and to torture and kill innocent people for their cause, then someone out there was still doing all those things.

A lack of social consensus had never stopped disturbed people from doing what they believed was right. If anything, hearing that they stood alone only amplified their intention, making them feel that they were right when they called themselves Messiah.

This, she suspected, was the case with Jotun. His behavior had become increasingly erratic. Though it was never bad enough to get him terminated, she had a log of all the unusual things he did from him muttering to himself under his breath (she caught snippets of something to the effect of "When I ascend, all this will change") to when he blankly stared at case files, sometimes for up to half an hour as he got lost in his own head.

While they were investigating him as leader of that order, they had no tangible evidence tying him to the organization, with the exception of the email that tipped them off to his leading it. Still, he was a person of interest in the 'Hounds' case, and her gut told her he had something to do with his own investigation, 'the Ghost,' as well. This 'Discord' was the only material witness for both. They couldn't risk her being placed in jeopardy by bringing her in and having Jotun realize that she had turned whistleblower.

They couldn't suspend or really investigate an agent without good cause. Internal affairs watched him, but that was the best she could hope for.

At least, they didn't have much cause until she slid the sketch from its envelope. The artist took the unified factors from each witness—those that each member reported—and made those into one drawing rather than present up to six different examples for the FBI to go off. Having six different sketches would've opened an untold number of possible suspects. Looking at the sheet in her hand, Garcia smiled, positive that now they only had one.

The face on the paper was that of her partner, Agent Theodore Jotun.

She felt her sidearm being drawn from its holster at approximately the same time someone struck her on the back of the head. Crying out, she fell forward, onto the island, rolling to the side and facing her attacker, but she was disoriented from the blow and stumbled into the countertop. Through her swimming vision, she saw Theo with a gun trained on her face.

"Did anyone ever tell you that you're a great detective?" His tone stayed calm and collected, the same way he might order a hot dog from a street vendor.

"You." Her only response fell flat as she gripped the edge of the counter, struggling against the encroaching darkness of the edges of her vision. Pain came in throbs, but she suppressed it by focusing on her erratic breathing.

"I can't let you get any closer to me. I can't let you stop me." A slight breathlessness between his words was the only indicator to what she knew, from experience, was a gradually growing state of excitement, fueled by delusion.

She kept her eyes focused on his gun, which shook slightly in his hand as a bead of something warm trickled down the back of her neck. "Do you think I'm trying to stop you?" Hands raised, she edged forward. "You're my partner; partners have to look out for each other, no matter what, which is why I applied to lead this investigation as soon as I heard you were being taken off it. At first, I wanted to make sure you were given credit if the case closed. The more we found...The more I wanted to be sure your mission was seen through to the end."

Having worked with all manner of psychos, addicts, and mental cases, she was used to this sort of fawning behavior that was required to coax people down from their grandiose mania. It was a tactic every agent was taught in basic training, but that was so long ago that Theo seemed not to recognize what she was doing. He was already so far gone that he could barely function as an agent anymore.

"My mission? Even if you were to try to stop me, you couldn't. I am the Incarnate. When my powers are returned to me, I will be unstoppable."

He lowered his gun just enough. Enough so that it wasn't

pointed at somewhere that, if shot, would lead to her death. Agent Garcia smiled. "I understand. I want to be a part of what you're doing. Please, let me help you. I know your followers were unfaithful. I will not be."

Eyeing her with a suspicious glare, he said, "Then I need you to tell me everything you know about where the Vessel is located, and where that little sidekick of his might be."

Nodding, she led him to her dining room, which, at the moment, functioned as a computer room since she had no plans for company. As he came up behind her, she spun back, twisting the gun out of his hand, but forgot about the one he took from her. While she raised her weapon toward his chest, he fired a round into her leg, causing her to stumble enough for him to dart forward, past the gun, and headbutt her. The blow left both of them with bloody noses, but he didn't seem to mind as he snatched the gun from her hand.

"Heathen," he said as he shot her in the chest, the bullet cracking through the sternum and ripping through her heart. She let out a faint, agonized gurgle as blood spurted from her mouth. Falling back, Garcia hit the floor, unable to speak, eyes wide and staring. She had enough time to look into her murderer's eyes before her own closed.

"All of you," he snarled. "Heathens and heretics, who'll rot upon my ascension."

Theo knew he'd need to know what she knew to act accordingly. Ignoring the blood dripping from his face, he took a seat at the table, mere feet from his ex-partner's body and the small crimson lake forming beneath her.

Booting up her computer, he found himself needing a password to access her files; he tried 'Jordan.' Everyone, even FBI agents, fall prey to the temptation to make easy passwords. Family member names were among the most common. Garcia, like most, made that mistake.

Soon, he stumbled onto an email thread between her and the director, discussing the internal affairs case—the one investigating him. The last was the most interesting.

Agent Garcia,

We can't remove him from operations yet. There isn't any tangible evidence. Suspicious behavior and one email aren't enough to bar an agent from service. Even the 'headquarters' for that cult proved a fruitless search. If he did once live there, he cleared out his belongings—and any trace of himself—long ago.

But if you insist he's responsible, set up a meeting with the informant. If she knows incriminating information, and has evidence, about Theodore, we can close two cases at once. Just make sure it's a real lead. Don't go chasing ghosts.

Sincerely,
Director D'Armillo

He opened the attachment and his emotions swung from outrage to elation. The details were for the next day, and there was an email address included. He could send her a message pretending to be Garcia, insisting on a morning meeting, telling the informant to text him where she was living 'for her own protection.'

Smiling to himself, he thought, *No one can stop me. No one.*

Chapter 32

Doing the laundry at a small spa was far from Skyler's most glamorous job, but it beat the constant hassle of working as a cashier. At least this way, she didn't have to deal with the obnoxious commentary of customers who didn't understand that expired coupons could not be used, food they had eaten could not be returned, and twelve items or less meant no, you could not go to the express lane with the fifty-plus items you were buying for your son's birthday party. Besides, the mind-numbing simplicity of the task gave her an opportunity to work through what she and Mark had been talking about, as well as plan their next move.

The plan had been to wait in their apartment until Jotun, the man who the FBI suspected was behind the order of Nyoru and was also the serial killer targeting Chelsea (even though she was positive it was him), came to attack them again. Without the Order, he would have to come after them himself, and when he did, the numerous video cameras she and Mark had set up would be able to document whatever happened there.

Discord said there was an internal affairs investigation going on since the bureau had no solid leads and tangible evidence. She and Mark had been offered the opportunity to speak with other agents and submit affidavits, but the killer had taken out people in protective custody before, often through poison. There was no way she was giving him the opportunity to get to her, especially when he could've recruited other agents as part of his cult.

Her phone vibrated, and opening it up, she saw a text from Discord: **Need to talk. Can you come by my place tonight?**

Another vibration, this one from Mark: **You get Discord's message?**

She texted back that she had, and that, since Discord hadn't tried to get in contact before, this must be really important. He agreed, saying they should go, as long as they were cautious. Skyler knew he still wasn't comfortable 'investigating' his own dad, but he had agreed to help because the man would be less dangerous behind bars.

Skyler texted Discord that they could, and she sent back an address and time. Replying that they'd be there, she slipped her phone into her pocket and continued her custodial duties.

A few minutes passed when a familiar voice chimed in her ear. "Excuse me, do you have any more small towels? I'm afraid my studio is a little low today."

"Sure." Skyler wondered if there'd be any recognition, given her weight loss, new hair, tan, and colored contacts. Handing a stack to Theresa, she smiled noncommittally, pretending not to know her. Theresa smiled and disappeared down an adjacent hallway.

That was lucky, she thought. *I don't want anyone else wrapped up in this.*

She continued throughout her day thinking this, grateful for the fact that Theresa had not recognized her. At least, that was what she thought until, just after punching out, Theresa approached her again.

"Skyler, right? You're the new assistant?" They were in the staff lounge, which was equipped with a couch, a TV, refrigerator, and Skyler's favorite amenity, a punch reader. It allowed her to slip in and out without people noticing. Usually.

She was off the clock, but still working.

"Yep, that's me. And you are?"

Glancing back over her shoulder, Theresa made sure no

one was approaching the lounge and shut the door. Her face said it all.

"I'm glad you're okay. I can't believe you didn't tell us the truth! We saw what happened on the news. The anchor said... said you were likely dead, since your car was at your house and...Well, you were missing."

Skyler ran a hand through her hair. It was hard enough to be a ghost, let alone one haunted by its own past.

"I...I didn't want to worry you. I didn't want you to get involved, to get hurt."

"We're your friends. Whether you like it or not, we were involved from the moment it happened. If you'd told us, we could've tried to help you, help you hide, helped you run, and you knew Jordan's sister is an FBI agent. Why, why leave?"

"Because I thought you wouldn't be my friends after." After months of lies, it felt good to tell the truth. "I've always been used to being on my own, to being the type of friend that people only keep around to use, the one constantly being called for help with their homework, fixing computers, study groups, projects. I figured, something as big as that, something that drastic...Any normal person would distance themselves from someone in my position."

Skyler turned her eyes to the floor, not wanting to risk seeing her friend cry, but Theresa stepped forward and wrapped her arms around her. "Well, I'm not going anywhere. Whatever you need, you let me know, and when all this is settled... When you don't have to hide who you are anymore, I'll be there for you. Just don't come back to folding towels." She smiled. "You're too smart for that."

Flashing back to Priscilla, Skyler stepped away, out of her friend's embrace.

"Don't get close to me. Not now, okay? The last time... didn't end well."

"What do you mean?"

"Theresa, Priscilla is gone. She got too close, tried to turn me over to the guy who was looking for me…The people who showed up killed her. Probably to keep her from talking later. Sorry." It was a lame ending, but she felt obligated to apologize. After all, Teresa and Priscilla had been close.

Theresa sighed, looking away. "Maybe that's for the better."

"For the…? You knew about her addiction?"

Giving a nod, Teresa gazed off into the distance. "I tried to help her, but she pushed me away. I figured she'd spend years wasting away, using more, working to afford her fix." She rubbed her hands against her Lycra pants. "To be killed that way is quick. Most would say she died young, maybe too young. But if her alternative was a slow and much more painful death, then that was mercy."

Skyler nodded. "Glad you agree. That's how I've felt."

"Still, I doubt your being here is an accident. Of all the places you wound up, you started working here, with me?"

There was no need to tell Teresa that Priscilla had been trying to find her, then Skyler's phone vibrated. Mark texted: **Getting late, where are you? Have to meet Discord.**

Tucking her phone away, Skyler said, "You're right. I must admit, the circumstances I've been through are a bit more than coincidental. And, on that note, there is somewhere I have to be. Don't worry. This time, I'll be sure to come back."

"I believe you." She smiled. "But…I sense something very powerful and very dark in your future. Whatever you do, promise me you'll be careful."

Skyler gave a soft, sad chuckle.

"I'll be as careful as I can be. I mean, I am being targeted by a serial killer, but I promise not to go base jumping in the meanwhile."

Exchanging another hug, Theresa said, "See you soon, my friend."

Skyler knew that no matter how this ended, they might never see each other again anyway. Saying goodbye was another blip on her emotional register. She'd miss Theresa, but it wouldn't hurt her nearly as much as it would hurt someone else.

"Yeah. Real soon."

She made her way to the door, disappearing into the hallway and then out of the building. The sun was beginning to set, the sky lit by a burst of colors that she knew would quickly be overwhelmed by darkness.

Chapter 33

Mark and Skyler pulled up outside an abandoned factory outside of the city. Discord's texts said they needed to meet in a nondescript, secure location, one to which they would not be tracked, so they'd come on guard. In times past, she'd always opted to meet in public, appearing as any ordinary person would. This seemed out of character. They'd come prepared, just in case something went wrong.

"You ready?" Mark stared up at the darkened structure, broken windows smudged with dirt looking back at them, like weary, cataract-ridden eyes.

Skyler walked forward, not bothering to respond aloud. If something was wrong, she definitely didn't want to give away their position by talking too much—not that the crunch of their feet over gravel and broken glass was quieter than speaking.

The inside of the building was vast and empty. It was clearly once used to house large equipment, likely the kind with conveyor belts and smelting chambers and a wide array of other loud, dangerous things, but the only remnant of such equipment was a series of chains hanging from the ceiling, the likes of which probably helped keep things in place. She didn't know enough about the manufacturing process to say for certain what anything might once have done. The walls were concrete and the walkways metal, letting out light clangs and loud creaks as the wind howled through the building.

Discord said to meet them in an administrative office on the second floor. Looking up, they saw a large box-shaped structure built into the second-floor walkway, so they crept up the nearby staircase and approached the office.

Moonlight streaming through the holes in the ceiling threw some light into the office, but the rest of it seemed darker by comparison. In the center, Discord knelt, head down, hands behind her back, a blindfold fixed over her eyes, a gag in her mouth. Skyler's chest constricted as she raced forward to pull the gag from her mouth. Discord began protesting quietly. Footsteps from behind them quickly overshadowed her muffled noises. Turning, they saw Theo approaching them, gun in his raised hand. It glinted as it passed through moonbeams.

"I knew," he seethed, both furious and delighted, "that I could trick you. I knew I could lure you out here with this—this traitor. Who are you to try to deny me my destiny?"

"Hello to you, too, Dad." Mark kept his voice steady and crossed his hands over his chest.

"Don't get smart with me. Never liked that about you. That mouth of yours."

Skyler spoke up. "Then what about me?"

She'd grown tired of running, and she didn't fear him anymore. Chelsea accepted her death when she looked at her parents' lifeless eyes. Now, whatever her name became, she'd accept his.

"Don't worry. The Saint of Glorious Pain will grant you solace in death, in exchange for the suffering of your life." He smiled, and when he did it was not mere moonlight glinting in his eyes. Rather than mania or lust, or a pathological need for violence like most serial killers displayed, she knew self-loathing fueled his rampage. He failed his wife, and needed to recreate her anguish, granting his sacrifices 'peace' through death. By killing the families first, he ensured that his victims were as desperate and depressed and afraid as his wife had been. That they were utterly without hope. By killing his victims, he rewrote his wife's death. He was there for her. He ended her pain. Rather than lonely suicide, murder became mercy.

To him, these deaths were his penance.

Like father, like son.

This same tormented need to fix the past also spurred Dave to take her along. The bartender, who couldn't remember his own real name, allowed her to skip town with him in an attempt to save his mother. The two had different ideas about what 'saving' meant.

Theo trained his gun on Mark. "Now, transfer the power to me. It is your destiny to let the Incarnate ascend to his full status."

"I'm not going to help you torture people. Just put the gun down. It's over."

Skyler stifled a laugh at the thought of this lost soul being even remotely close to a god. While the gunman was distracted, she helped Discord to her feet, snaking a switchblade from her back pocket. She cut the woman's bonds away. The informant cupped a hand to her ear.

"All texts on my phone are copied to Agent Garcia. She should have this place surrounded."

"You should learn to whisper quieter," Jotun said with a derisive snort. "Besides, Garcia is dead. We're all alone here."

"Dad, put the gun down."

Turning on his son again, Jotun glared and waved the gun around. "Not until the transference is complete. I *will* become that which I was destined to be."

So many spend their lives running from destiny, Chelsea, or Skyler, or whoever, thought. *It's almost noble he wants to embrace it. If only his idea of fate wasn't fueled by PTSD and a possible psychotic episode.* She inwardly shrugged. No fixing those who don't want to be fixed.

"Even if I knew how, you can't make me, so give up."

Outrage overwhelmed him. Then a dark smile overtook his face, and he spoke in a voice smoother than a blade between two ribs. "Actually, I *can* make you."

Moving his arm slightly, he pulled the trigger, sending a

round through Skyler's chest, below her left collar bone. She felt the bullet twist as it shredded through muscle and nerves, sending a spray of blood as it went straight through her. The exit wound would be bigger, more painful, and harder to heal, but at the moment, all she cared about was the juxtaposition of cool air against the red-hot edges of the hole the bullet left behind. Anatomy hadn't been her strong suit, but she knew a severed artery when she felt it. Stumbling back, she began to fall. Discord caught her and kept her head from banging off the ground. The knife flew from her hand, clattering near Mark's feet. Someone yelled but she could only distinctly hear a gunshot, echoing.

Mark stared, wide-eyed, for as long as he could manage before snapping his lids shut and turning to his father. He growled, "For my entire life, I've tried to give you credit where it wasn't due. I tried to convince myself that you were a good father, a good man, someone who did all he could and couldn't do enough. Someone who wanted to change this world for the better. But now, I see you're nothing but a madman who enjoys pain. You can't get enough of it. Guess we're not so different, though. I spent my life trying to fix everyone else's mistakes. Trying to heal the whole world. Well, I'm leaving that duty to someone else."

He reached down, grabbing the knife that had landed mere inches from his feet. Before his father could react—before he could flinch or hesitate or second guess—he held the knife to his temple, dragging the blade sideways across his face. He screamed, keeping steady despite the pain, cutting his own eyes out, not stopping the motion until the tip of the knife reached his other temple.

Theodore screamed, watching decades of work bleed onto the floor. The religion he'd built, the lives he'd ended, every stepping-stone on the path to becoming the Saint of Glorious Pain, unfeeling and undeniable, fell away. Enraged, he stomped forward, kicking Mark to the ground.

"Damn you! Stupid, stupid boy!" he shouted. "You kill your mother, and I spend my whole life trying to ensure nobody ever has to die like she did, trying to become a god so I could decide who sinks into that abyss, save the good people from depression and inflict torment on the criminals and scum that walk these streets, and you end it? How are you so selfish that you could deny my rightful power? My duty to dispense solace and suffering?"

In all his focused rage, he hadn't noticed the footsteps coming toward him until they'd stepped over Mark, into striking distance. A hand swung, knocking his gun away, down onto the floor below. Her other hand locked around his jaw, forcing him to make eye contact.

Chelsea held his gaze, eyes mirrored, locking him in place. "That duty isn't yours."

He stared back into himself as she emptied every last vestige of pain in her heart into his.

"All the people you killed, all those you had Discord torture, all the suffering you caused will now be yours to bear. But I take all the fond memories you've ever had; from the day you were born to this very instant. Every fleeting glimpse of peace, of joy, of love, of hope. I will leave you with *nothing*. But I refuse to kill you. I leave you to a long, agonizing death as your guilt rips you apart from within. You will know the despair of a life without light. I leave you to your own darkness. I leave you to your ruin."

All that astral anatomy she'd stored filled him to bursting, years of isolation, heartache, and abuse exploding through Theo's mind like a steel drum, sending fire and shrapnel in all directions, lighting up his nerves and shredding through his reality. In its wake, she tore every ounce of hope from his soul, every thread of joy in his memories unraveling. His scream, born of agony transmuting into physical pain, resonated around the empty room as he stumbled back against a rotted-out guardrail. The metal gave way and he fell, dropping the gun on the catwalk, his legs shattering on impact with the cold ground.

Blood poured down Mark's face. He saw nothing, but heard his father hit the ground. With his eyes went his 'gift,' and the sound of Theo's bones breaking was the snap of a deadbolt locking his dark past away.

Discord grabbed her blindfold, slipping it over his face.

"I'm not sure if this is sterile, but it'll help stem the bleeding. I...I think."

Letting out a pained gasp, he put on the blindfold. Sanitary or no, it was better than his hands and the dust-and-dirt-filled air. Discord knelt by his side, staring up at Chelsea. Their gazes met. Chelsea held her there, then let her go, neither giving nor taking.

"I think we all have questions." Chelsea knelt by Mark's side. "We'll have to save the answers for later."

Somewhere below, a woman yelled, "FBI! Hands in the air!"

Theo cried out, his wail turning to a sob.

"We're up here!" Discord yelled. "We need a medic!"

She had no idea what the protocol was for a man who cut his eyes out of his own head, but she imagined it'd take a small army of doctors to help them—not that he'd ever get his sight back. Not organically, at any rate.

Mark cleared his throat. "When this is over, I say we grab a drink. All of us, as friends. Use our real names. Real IDs. Hell, I hope I get carded." He chuckled as red rivers poured down around his lips.

Chelsea laughed. "First round's on you."

Two paramedics reached them, so Discord and Chelsea backed away. They helped Mark to his feet, escorting him down to the ambulance. Another paramedic offered to give the women a ride to the hospital, but they refused, following along in the car Chelsea left in the parking lot. They didn't have to speak or acknowledge each other at all. Discord spoke anyway.

"I did...horrible things. You know that, don't you?" It

wasn't really a question.

"I do." Chelsea kept her eyes straight on the road.

"So, are you going to...you know, like Theo?"

She laughed. "You acted out of fear for your own life. I've seen everything you're holding onto. Theo would've killed them anyway. Besides, you're punishing yourself enough."

Discord looked up at a star-filled sky, moving a hand to block the flashing glare of the ambulance lights in front of them.

"You'll need a new name though. Discord doesn't quite suit you anymore."

"Maybe...Do I call you Nyoru, then?"

"Ugh! No, please don't *ever*. Stupid dramatic crap. I'm still Chelsea."

With a faint flicker of hope, she said, "What about the Saint?"

The ambulance made a sharp turn into the city proper, and they were at a hospital moments later. She focused on driving until they arrived, but once Mark vanished into an emergency room, the nurses came to talk to them.

"He's lost a lot of blood," said a nurse, Jewel, whose crinkled eyes made it clear the situation wasn't looking good.

Still, Chelsea smiled at Discord, then back at the nurse.

"He'll be okay, I think. He's got a Saint watching over him."

Epilogue

The Empty Vessel needed a name for admissions purposes. Chelsea made a phone call to Jordan, who now worked in the Bureau, and found his birth name was Jared Porya, after his mother's maiden name. They talked for a while after, about Talia, about these cases, about the fact that Theo would die in federal prison, and good riddance to him.

Chelsea didn't reveal the full truth, obviously. Wasn't the time for that yet. She did mention having 'pushed' Theo over the edge, resulting in his paralysis. Jordan couldn't have sounded happier if she tried.

"So, I'm not getting arrested?" Chelsea asked.

"Please. When I'm done here, you'll get a medal."

She doubted a rookie agent could arrange that, but still, it felt pretty good.

As for Jared, they didn't even try to save his sight. Didn't seem to bother him much. He recovered quickly, smiling more than she'd ever seen before.

He'd been released from the hospital a week earlier, and now he, Chelsea, and Symphony sat around a table in Chelsea's apartment. Why skip town again with no one chasing after them?

They were waiting on some people though, and soon came a knock at the door. Chelsea jumped up, showing Theresa and Jordan into the apartment. They wore the same casual clothes and wary expressions, but soon relaxed when they saw that, despite everything suggesting she should be a traumatized wreck, their old friend was perfectly fine.

"Welcome to my apartment! I can actually afford it now that I'm living under my own name and can, you know, access my inheritance."

"Yeah, are you sure you're okay?" Jordan cocked her head.

"I'm not exactly thrilled it happened, but silver linings, right? If we don't at least *try* to see the good, we only see the bad."

Theresa nodded. "What a good mindset! But I think we're missing some introductions." She looked over toward Symphony and Jared.

"Of course! So sorry." She went through introductions, and once she pointed out that, beneath his blindfold, this was Dave the Bartender, recognition crashed over them. They didn't recognize Symphony, of course. She'd cut her hair, doing away with the stained braid in favor of a spiky, shoulder-length cut, but the tips stayed blood red. Nobody could quite resolve that issue, but she stuck with her minimalist color scheme. It seemed to work. At least she hadn't had anyone ask, *Is that blood?*

They sat around the table, each with a glass in hand, sharing a bottle of Lagavulin twelve year that Jared insisted on buying. His way of saying thanks for being freed from a life of occult servitude.

"Are you sure you should be drinking?" Theresa asked him.

"I'm going to crash into things even if I'm sober, so I might as well celebrate, right?"

That seemed rational enough.

Chelsea raised her glass. "A toast, if I may." They all nodded. "It can seem wrong to celebrate when we've lost someone we care about. Whether a sister," she looked at Jordan, "or a friend," she looked at Theresa, "or a parent. Even an abusive one." She looked at Jared.

"I know the people who love us wouldn't want us to grieve too long or too deeply. Pain is the snare that squeezes life from even the healthiest of us, and I for one prefer the company of the living to memories of the dead. So, thank you, all of you, for being here. There is so much to this world, and all of us here have barely scratched the surface."

One by one, she locked onto everyone but Jared, maintaining eye contact and showing her power, ensuring her friends wouldn't think she'd simply gone insane. They sat back, stunned, unsure of what to say, knowing Chelsea wasn't just Chelsea anymore.

"Many choose to live in the tiny little bubble of their immediate reality, but I'm going to test this world's limits, for better and for worse. I am both the snowflake and the avalanche. Join me, or don't. The choice is yours. The future, however, is mine."

The Saint of Glorious Pain downed her drink, savoring the way it burned.

Acknowledgements

Well, I owe a lot of people a lot of things, so let's hope my debt collector accepts this as a form of payment. Kidding.

In seriousness, I'll start with the obvious: I'd like to thank my parents, without whom I wouldn't have been possible, and my wife, Andrea, without whom this book wouldn't have been possible. I may have written it before you came into my story, but you kept me going when I wasn't able to on my own, and this book wouldn't have come out if you hadn't been there. Also, thank you to my sister, Rhea. You're smarter and funnier than you realize.

I'd like to thank the whole brood of chickens I raised while writing this book for keeping my personal life full of levity and life. Tina, Fuzzy, I'm sorry the racoon got you. Nugget, Empress, I'm sorry your new owner wasn't able to save you from heat stroke when I couldn't take care of you anymore. Psycho, you're still alive. Good job! Keep screaming, you weirdo.

I'm going to delve into narcissism and thank myself, for all I am, and all the people I have ever been, with all the names I've written under, and all the stories I've lost to time and shoddy memory. I didn't get here without you, first.

But most of all, thank you, A. M. Rycroft. I almost buried this book in the back of a hard drive in my closet and forgot all about it, so this literally wouldn't have come together if you hadn't given me the prod to get back to doing what I'm here to do when stress and illness took me out of commission.

About the Author

Kira Blackwood has written many things under many names. *The Mirrors by Which I End the World* is her first major work under this one. She's also died at least once, maybe four or five times, depending on who you ask. Her work is as unapologetic and weird as she is. Don't ask her about raising pet chickens unless your schedule's clear. When she isn't writing, she can be found in cold places, the gym, or honking at geese.

Excerpt from *In Case of Carnage* by Gerry Griffiths

1
CASE NUMBER: 18-01-236

Clare Carver placed her bulky forensic kit by the body, avoiding the pool of blood inches away from Detective Bill Hendrix's patent leather shoes. He observed her methodical process, jotting down specifics in his notepad.

The victim was a teenage girl, possible runaway. Skin smooth as Philadelphia cream cheese. Black Hot Topic T-shirt with a crudely cut hole haloing a green barbell belly button ring. Designer blue jeans fashionably snipped away at the knees. Red Keds high-tops without shoelaces. Green spiked hair in the rust-colored blood on the cement floor.

Bill crouched to inspect the weepy quarter-inch hole in her forehead, the gold shield on his belt digging into his gut. He noticed puncture marks on the girl's neck, just under her right ear.

"Are those incisor wounds on her throat?"

Clare leaned forward for a closer look. "Possibly."

"Too clean for an animal bite."

"What are you suggesting?"

"I'd say it's the work of a vampire."

Clare gave him an incredulous look before bursting into laughter.

"Better not let Hank hear you say that." Clare glanced at Bill's gun. "Is that a snub-nosed thirty-eight?"

"Smith and Wesson. Same as Hank carries. Why?"

"They still make those? When are you guys going to get with the latest department issue?"

"What, those plastic guns? No thanks." Bill shook his head, noting Clare's firearm strapped to her side.

Clare pulled her handgun with slick precision. "You're looking at a Glock 29 ten-millimeter with a ten-round clip, polymer frame, and non-corrosive coating, so it won't rust like those pea-shooters you two call guns," she bragged before holstering her weapon. "Standard issue, per the captain."

"Hey, a *lot* of famous detectives carried thirty-eights. *Dragnet's* Sergeant Joe Friday, Jim Rockford in *The Rockford Files*."

"Bill, those guys weren't even real cops. Please don't tell me you're packing those three-eighty automatics around your ankles."

"They're great little backup guns."

"Next you're going to tell me you use speedloaders." She laughed, patting the two ten-round clips on her belt next to the tactical folding knife in a Velcro sheath beside her holstered high-tech semi-automatic.

Bill was about to reach into his jacket pocket when a mall security guard came into the room looking like he had just left his mother's funeral.

"What are you two squabbling about?" Detective Hank Jenkins entered the storeroom right behind the despondent security guard. Hank slipped the man's firearm in an evidence bag.

"Where's Silverman?" Bill asked. Normal protocol required that the first uniformed officer on the crime scene be present to answer questions during the primary investigation.

"Other side of the mall. Checking surveillance."

"Bill thinks the girl was bitten by a vampire." Clare pointed at the dead girl's neck.

"Jeez, Bill. Can't you be serious for one minute?"

The disgruntled mall guard glanced at the dead girl, then stared down at his boots. "I can't believe it. I take this lousy job to subsidize my pissant retirement, and look what happens."

"Bill, this is Ralph Talbert," Hank said.

Bill nodded at the security guard.

Hank said to Ralph, "Tell my partner what you told me."

Ralph cleared his throat. "The last few days there have been a number of break-ins in the mall."

Bill asked, "Why didn't the mall manager report them?"

"Maybe he was in on it. I don't know."

"Go on."

"They cut the padlocks on the metal gates, crawl under and jimmy the entry doors. So far, they've broken into about eight different stores."

Bill asked, "What are they after?"

"Well, it's weird. This mall's got tons of electronics stores, stuff you could make good money selling at the flea market. These guys? They take clothes. They've even raided the kitchens in the food court."

"How are they getting into the mall if the outside doors are locked?"

"Personally, I think it's an employee who has access to a master key." Ralph glanced over at the dead girl. "I swear, one of them was pointing a gun at me."

Hank asked, "What do you mean, 'one of them'?"

"There were two."

Hank gave Ralph a hard stare.

Ralph shrugged. "Jesus, I thought I told you."

A loud crash came from the main floor of the sporting goods store.

"What was that?" Bill snatched his gun out of the shoulder rig.

Hank stuffed Ralph's gun into the side pocket of his coat. He drew his .38 snub-nosed out of the holster clipped to his belt.

Clare threw back the slide on her Glock.

Hank and Bill went first. Clare stepped out next with Ralph trailing behind her.

The sporting goods showroom was cast in shadows. A majority of the overhead fluorescent panels were turned off to conserve energy.

Hank spotted movement to his right. He signaled Bill and Clare.

A scrawny teenager stood in front of a smashed display case, shoving small boxes into a rucksack.

"Let's see those hands!" Bill barked. "This is the—"

The kid swiveled around with a shotgun. The muzzle flash lit up as the boom thundered in the room. Bill shoved Clare to the floor and dove on top of her. Pumping another cartridge into the chamber, the gunman swung the barrel and blasted again. A rack of sleeping bags exploded in a goose down blizzard.

Hank fired a quick shot, striking the kid in the shoulder. The impact sent him toppling into the display case.

Bill got up. Clare sprang to her feet.

"I only winged him," Hank cautioned.

The teenage boy lay on the floor amid ammunition boxes covered with glass shards. Hank kicked the shotgun out of the kid's reach. Bill and Clare kept their guns trained on the suspect.

"Please don't kill me," the kid begged.

"You're lucky we didn't." Bill grabbed the shotgun off the floor.

"Wait a minute. You're not them."

"Who did you *think* we were?"

"Aw man, you're the cops!"

"Hey, where's Ralph?" Hank turned, scouting the store for the security guard.

"Over there." Clare pointed.

Ralph was dead on the floor, sprawled under the glow of a ceiling light. His face was a bloody pulp, riddled with buckshot, looking like the inside of a pomegranate.

Hank stared at the wounded teenager. "You screwed up big time, son."

Bill bent down to scrutinize the boy. "He's got the same bite marks on his neck as the girl."

A red blossom bloomed on the boy's shirt. The bullet had struck the right deltoid a couple of inches away from the shoulder.

Clare holstered her Glock. "I need to stop the bleeding." She took a pair of blue gloves out of her pants pocket. She stretched the elastic before slipping them on. "Hand me one of those shirts for a compress."

Bill grabbed a shirt off a rack. Clare wadded it up and placed it over the wound. She took the boy's left hand and pressed it palm-side down on the compress. "What's your name?"

"Peter."

"Okay, Peter. Keep applying pressure."

Clare glanced down at the boy's right arm. "Guys, look at this."

Two puncture marks on the forearm, too large for needle tracks.

"Jesus, Peter," Clare said, "Who did this to you?"

"The vampires."

Hank shook his head. "Kid, you're in enough trouble. What are you even doing in here?"

"We thought it would be cool to hide out in the mall after it closed."

"When was that?"

"I don't know. A week ago?"

Hank saw the surprised looks on Bill and Clare's faces. "Weren't you afraid of getting caught?"

"We'd smoked a bunch of weed."

"So who's your girlfriend?"

"Sissy."

"Tell us about the bite marks."

Peter must have pressed too hard on his wound because he crinkled up his face. "They feed on us. I'm a donor. Sissy's a blood doll. They take turns, pass us around like a bottle of Jim Beam."

"So you and Sissy broke into those stores?"

"Yes, they made us."

Hank frowned. "What do you mean, 'made you'? Sounds to me like you could have escaped any time you wanted."

"They have my sister. They're holding her hostage. If we don't do what they want, they'll kill her."

"What's your sister's name?"

"Peg. We needed the gun to rescue her."

"How many of these . . ." Hank paused, rolling his eyes at Bill, "*Vampires* would you say there are?"

"Four. I'm telling you, they're crazy." Peter's eyes widened. "These guys are stronger than shit!" He raised his head off the floor to gaze around. "Hey, where's Sissy?"

Bill broke the news. "Your girlfriend is dead. The guard you killed shot her."

Peter scrunched his eyes shut, tears leaking down his cheeks.

Hank asked, "Where are they keeping your sister?"

"Under the mall."

"How do we find her?"

"Follow the corridor at the food court to the restrooms. The 'Employees Only' door to the right of the men's room is unlocked. Take the stairs down to the basement. There's a huge tunnel the delivery trucks use. Go right until you see a big 'W2' stenciled on the wall to your left with a black door. Their hideout is in there."

Bill scowled. "You know, we have a problem."

Hank let out a sigh. "And what is that?"

"They're vampires."

"This is a bunch of bull."

"You know bullets won't kill them."

"My Glock will," Clare chimed in.

"That might slow them down a bit"—Bill raised his eyebrows—"until the lead pops out of their bodies. There're only four ways you can kill a vampire." He counted them off on his fingers. "Drive a stake through their heart, cut off their head, expose them to sunlight, or set them on fire."

"I can't believe I'm standing here listening to this nonsense," Hank said. "Let's go find these jokers."

Clare used her cell phone to call the security office. She told Officer Silverman to get back to the sporting goods store, on the double to watch Peter. She then called dispatch to summon an ambulance and notify the captain of their situation. Hank handcuffed Peter's right hand to a pole next to the display case.

"Don't move. Someone will be here shortly." Clare stripped off her gloves.

They hustled out of the sporting goods store and dashed down the wide corridor that separated the specialty shops. Officer Silverman was already jogging in their direction and gave them a wave.

After reaching the food court, they headed for the restrooms. Hank spotted the door: Employees Only. It was unlocked, so he pushed it open. Cement stairs stretched down into the tenebrous gloom of the underground tunnels. He started down, Bill a step behind, Clare taking up the rear.

Halfway down, Hank heard a crack. He glanced over his shoulder. "What was that?"

Bill held up what looked like a stick.

"Is that an arrow?"

"Yeah, I broke off the metal tip."

"Why?"

"The shaft has to be made solely of wood when driven through a vampire's heart."

Hank looked at what Bill had in his other hand. "You took a crossbow?"

"Yeah, I grabbed it on our way out of the store, along with some arrows." Bill pulled another arrow out of the short quiver that was sticking out of the side pocket of his jacket. He pressed the end against the concrete wall, snapping the tip off.

"Jesus, I don't believe you!" Hank continued down.

Clare tapped Bill on the shoulder. "Jeez, Bill. You're really serious about this."

"Clare, they're vampires."

"You know, it might not hurt to have a little chat with the departmental shrink."

"Why? 'Cause you're dating him?"

"No, I'm not!"

"Not what *I* heard."

"Okay, we went out *once*, but—"

Hank barked from the bottom of the stairs, "Will you two keep it down!"

Clare and Bill rushed down the steps and joined Hank. They stood in the middle of a large tunnel with loading docks stretching in both directions, tapering into the darkness.

"The only way to gain access from the outside is through one of those entrances, which are controlled by the guard in the security office." Hank pointed to an automatic roll-up door.

The tunnel was nearly twenty feet high—wide enough for two big rig trailers to squeeze past each other going in opposite directions. A network of yellow globe lights, various-sized plumbing pipes, and conduits of electrical wiring ran along the ceiling. The nearest loading dock had the store's name stenciled on the side of the concrete ramp.

Farther on they found the black door next to the large "W2" painted on the wall. Hank stood on one side of the door, one hand on the handle. Bill and Clare steeled themselves against the wall.

Hank flung open the door. They stormed in—Hank sweeping left, Clare taking the right, and Bill up the middle—panning their guns about the large room. It looked like a den for the homeless. Filthy sleeping bags were strewn across the floor. Black garbage bags bulged with stolen merchandise. Empty food containers were tossed in a corner. Trash was scattered everywhere. The stale, putrid air reeked of body odor and filthy clothes.

The room was deserted.

"Maybe they heard the gunshots." Bill kicked a shoebox across the floor.

"I heard something!" Clare bolted out of the room. The two detectives charged out after her.

"There they are!" Clare pointed to two figures racing down the tunnel.

A scream came from the opposite direction.

"Damn, they split up," Hank said. "Bill, Clare, go that way. I'll follow these two."

* * *

They were faster than a pair of doped-up track runners. The way they ran reminded Hank of apes loping in the jungle. The sounds of their feet slapping the pavement let him know they were barefoot. Probably didn't have time to put on shoes. He wondered if they were armed.

His legs were already starting to burn. He needed to get back to his routine morning jogs, devote fewer hours behind the desk.

Hank slowed as he reached a bend in the tunnel. If they

were smart, they would wait in ambush, attack when he came running blindly around the corner.

He stopped for a second to listen. He could hear air flowing through the ducts above his head, liquid surging down the pipes. Somewhere behind the walls, machines hummed, busy at work.

Hank slid along the concrete wall, edging around the bend. He found himself standing below the loading dock with the sporting goods store logo.

A forklift was parked on one side of the huge platform. Empty pallets were stacked high against a wall near a control panel for a giant gray compactor—the kind for flattening cardboard boxes. The twin doors remained open on the hopper, like crushing jaws waiting for a victim.

Half a dozen pallets stood in front of the closed door of the receiving area with merchandise covered in shrink-wrap. Hank pointed his .38, climbing the short flight of concrete steps leading to the platform. He crept past the forklift to the first pallet.

He could see the labels through the shrink-wrap: boxed camping stoves and cases of kerosene. He squeezed between two more pallets stacked high with boxes. It was like being wedged inside a narrow passage. A pallet skidded toward Hank, threatening to crush him against the pallet directly behind him.

He was shocked to see the forklift parked, unmanned, on the other side of the loading dock. Hank escaped from between the pallets before they slammed together.

A hulking figure stood only five feet away.

Hank closed his eyes briefly, thinking he was seeing things. When he reopened them, it was still standing there.

Maybe Bill was right. Maybe they *did* exist.

The only vampire Hank had ever seen was on the cover of a DVD case Bill had shown him to persuade him to take the movie home to watch. The vampire? Bela Lugosi, creepy with his sinister stare and lecherous grin, but still resembling a man.

Not *this* vampire.

Two short, stubby horns jutted from its forehead, its head smooth and hairless. Its face and scalp were inked with swirling, weird symbols and stars. Its eyebrows, both sides of its nose, lips, and even its chin, were pierced with rings and metal studs. Its earlobes were grotesquely enlarged with black disks. Its eyes were shaded with mascara, and its pupils were eerie, thin slits against green serpentine irises.

It stood about five-ten, wearing a tight-fitting black T-shirt and dark jeans. Its bulging muscles were a roadmap of ropy veins ready to burst, rippling like those of a bodybuilder on steroids.

The vampire opened its mouth, giving Hank a preview of things to come.

Hank couldn't believe the size of its fangs. Every tooth had been filed to a tiny point, and its tongue was forked like a serpent's.

"Don't move! You're under arrest!" Hank reached under his jacket for his handcuffs when the vampire charged.

Hank fired two quick rounds, nailing the bloodsucker in the chest.

The vampire didn't even flinch. It looked down at the bullet holes in its T-shirt. It dabbed some blood with its finger, ran the tip over its tongue.

Hank aimed for the thing's ugly head and pulled the trigger.

The bullet grazed the side of the vampire's skull, clipping off a horn. Blood gushed out and down its face. The vampire ran across the loading dock, one hand clamped on its head.

"Stop!" Hank shouted.

The vampire vaulted onto the rim of the compactor's hopper. It was about to jump up onto the main housing when Hank fired again.

The bullet struck the vampire in the leg, causing it to tumble into the hopper.

Hank ran over. "Give it up!" He kept his gun trained on the creature. He warily approached until he was within a foot.

The vampire lunged, its long, sharp nails piercing Hank's jacket. One powerful yank slammed him up against the steel wall of the hopper.

The vampire glared, flicking its tongue.

Hank reached back with one hand, his fingers fumbling blindly on the control panel. He punched the red button.

The hopper motor rumbled, then roared. The twin doors began their slow descent to crush the contents of the bin.

Instead of trying to escape the hopper, the vampire started to drag Hank over the rim.

Hank hooked the toe of his shoe under a lip of metal near the floor, anchoring himself. He grabbed the metal face to push back. The vampire refused to budge.

Hank shot the vampire's hand that was clutching his jacket. The bullet ripped through the palm, blowing out a bloody chunk from the back of its hand. Its grip relaxed, enabling Hank to pull free—just as the heavy doors came down on the fiend's neck. The pistons pushed the doors deep inside the hopper like a guillotine, decapitating the vampire.

Hank hit the red button, switching off the machine.

A hand gripped Hank's shoulder, hoisted him in the air, and threw him fifteen feet across the loading dock. The security guard's gun fell out of his pocket. His service revolver clattered across the concrete loading dock.

Another vampire skulked from behind the pallets, its face the spitting image of the one dead in the hopper.

* * *

Bill and Clare were on the far side of the underground passage when they heard the first shots.

"Do you think Hank's okay?" Clare slowed down to glance back.

"Hank can take care of himself."

They edged around a bend in the tunnel.

"Where'd they go?" Clare aimed her Glock, ready for anything.

They stood in the middle of the thoroughfare between two loading docks.

Bill craned his neck to look up. "Careful, they could be—"

A woman screamed on the loading dock to their right.

"Cover me." Bill dashed up the concrete steps.

When he reached the top, a muscular creep with facial tattoos—*Christ, are those horns?*—and black clothing held a teenage girl hostage.

"Let the girl go!" Bill loaded an arrow into the crossbow. "Are you Peg?"

The girl hitched a breath, unable to speak. The vampire laughed when it saw Bill's weapon. With one hand, it wrapped its fingers around Peg's neck and raised her off her feet.

Bill leveled the crossbow. The creature glared, revealing razor-point fangs, and laughed. Bill took his shot. The vampire bellowed when the arrow buried itself into its right shin. It dropped the girl. Peg scampered toward Bill.

He cocked back the bowstring and slipped another arrow into the crossbow. He waited for Peg to get out of his line of fire, then pulled the trigger. The arrow sailed to the right of the vampire.

The vampire flew at Bill. It grabbed the detective, baring its fangs. It bit through his jacket clear down to the flesh of his shoulder.

"Son of a—" Bill reached down, jiggled the arrow in the vampire's shin. The vampire howled, shoving Bill back. Bill snatched another arrow from the quiver in his pocket. He drove the jagged tip into the vampire's heart.

The vampire gasped, flailing back its arms. It landed on

the hard cement with a heavy thud.

Bill looked at the trembling teenager. "You're safe now." He staggered over to the edge of the loading dock. "Clare! I've got the girl!"

But Clare was gone.

[...]

Visit our website (www.epic-publishing.com/books) for more information on buying your copy of *In Case of Carnage*.